Don't Open Your Eyes

D1438117

Ann Halam is the pen name of Gwyneth Jones. She was born and raised in Manchester, and after graduating from Sussex University spent some years travelling throughout South East Asia. She now lives in Brighton with her husband and son. As well as being a children's author, Ann Halam writes adult science fiction and fantasy books, as Gwyneth Jones.

Other books by the same author from Orion

The Haunting of Jessica Raven
The Fear Man
The Powerhouse
Crying in the Dark
The N.I.M.R.O.D. Conspiracy

Don't Open Your Eyes

Ann Halam

Dolphin Paperbacks

First published in Great Britain in 2000
as a Dolphin paperback
by Orion Children's Books
a division of the Orion Publishing Group Ltd
Orion House
5 Upper St Martin's Lane
London WC2H 9EA

A catalogue record for this book is available from the British Library

Typeset at The Spartan Press Ltd,
Lymington, Hants
Printed in Great Britain by The Guernsey Press Co. Ltd,
Guernsey, C.I.

ISBN 1 85881 791 9

One

Diesel found Herbie the squirrel lying on the ironing board, in the middle of a mass of boxes and newspaper padding and upturned chairs; and carried him around with her. Up the stairs and down the stairs, her footsteps sounding loud and strange on the dusty bare wood. Soon 57 Linden Grove would be a house with people living in it. Now it was still empty and strange, promising secrets. She looked into her own new bedroom, her parents' room, the spare room, the nice big bathroom. In the bathroom she found her mum putting up their yellow shower curtain with the stars on it. 'Are you doing anything useful?' said Mum.

'I'm settling in.'

Mum nodded, and didn't seem bothered. If it was important to get the shower curtain up, it was just as important for someone to walk around cuddling a soft toy, thinking *this house is ours now, this is where we live . . .* Diesel's parents had talked about getting a proper house with a proper garden for years and years. She had shared the dream for as long as she could remember. She had pictures in her memory-box that she had drawn when she was five years old – with trees that looked like green

1

lollipops, and human beings that were triangles or rectangles, with round heads and crooked legs sticking out at odd angles – titled Our New House. The house in those pictures – a triangle on top of a square, with a curly pig's tail of smoke sticking out of a chimneypot – had never happened. There had always been something in the way, either not enough money or no houses of the right kind to be found. Now the dream was real.

She looked down from the window of her new bedroom into their new back garden. It had a long rectangle of tufty lawn, untidy flower borders; and a greenhouse at the bottom. The garden of the empty house next door was more interesting. She could see into it over the wall. There were full-grown trees growing there, far too big for a back garden. Through their branches she could see things lurking, like shipwrecks on the green seabed of grass and weeds. Old furniture, and wasn't that a supermarket trolley? And maybe parts of a motor bike? She decided she would investigate. It didn't look as if it would be hard to climb over.

She could hear the removal men having trouble with the sofa, so she went to the top of the stairs to see what was happening. Diesel's dad was hopping around, giving the men advice. The men were not taking the advice, and seemed to be enjoying the game of knocking as much paint as they could from the walls and the woodwork in the front hall.

'I'll tell you what we need to do,' said the foreman. 'We need to take it round the back, and in from the garden through those french doors. We'll have to knock up the neighbours.'

Everyone went outside – four removal men, Diesel's

dad, Diesel and Herbie – and looked at the houses on either side of number 57. 'Don't think we want to knock there,' muttered the foreman. He meant number 55, the empty house with the jungle for a garden. It looked as neglected in front as it did at the back. The small front yard held a heap of rubble, some festering litter, and an old armchair.

'It's empty,' said Diesel's dad. 'I'll have to get on to the Council about that chair.'

So they rang the bell at number 59. Diesel and her mum and dad had met the people who lived there: Mrs Michael, the houseproud old white lady and her son. It was the middle-aged son who was called Michael. Diesel's family didn't yet know their proper surname. Michael was out at work. His mother was happy to let them take the sofa through her house. The removal men went in to have a look, and it was okay. They wouldn't have to deal with the awkward corner that made the front hall in number 57 difficult, so through they went. Diesel came and watched, hoping the men wouldn't bash Mrs Michael's beautiful clean paintwork too badly. Everything in number 59 was shining and immaculate.

Dad said to Mrs Michael, 'I'm not very happy about having an empty house next door. It's a liability. Property that isn't being looked after can get problems, like damp, and there's no one to notice it or fix it. In an old terrace, that soon means trouble for the houses on either side. There's no For Sale board. Do you know what's going on?'

'Oh, number 55 isn't empty,' said the old lady, as if Dad must have known this.

'It isn't empty? You're kidding. I'm sure it's empty.'

3

'The boys live there, the Knight boys. With their mother, except if she's off on one of her sprees. The father left them years ago, of course.'

Diesel saw her dad's face fall. It was quite a change – one second happy and excited, eyes sparkling; next second all shocked.

'I really think the estate agent told us that 55 was standing empty.'

'Well, I don't know what they told you,' said Mrs Michael. 'But it's not.'

Mrs Michael was as clean as her house. She wore a pink nylon overall, brown stockings and floral slippers with a pink furry trim. Every time Diesel had seen her she'd been wearing the same kind of thing, usually with pink rubber gloves as well: and she'd been holding a can of polish and a cloth or something. Her hair was set in gleaming white curls, and she was wearing lipstick and powder, very neatly applied, though she was obviously just doing the housework. The first time the Pragers had come to look at number 57, Mrs Michael had popped out into her own garden when they were out at the back, and talked to them over the wall; which was much lower than the wall on the number 55 side, and topped by a fence that had roses trained over it. She had chatted to them through the bare branches of the roses (it had been winter then), and they had all three felt that they were being checked out as possible neighbours. She'd been friendly every time they'd come back since, so she must have decided they were okay. Diesel thought Mrs Michael was *too* clean, too pink-and-white. A younger Diesel – she'd always been accident prone – might have had problems with someone like that living next door. Balls over walls, noisy games, broken windows sort of bother. But she was fourteen now, so she expected she could keep out of trouble.

In all the chats they'd had with Mrs Michael and her son, they had never talked about number 55, the house the Pragers had believed was empty. It just hadn't come up.

The removal men took down a section of the fence where there was a gap between the roses, and the sofa went through into the Pragers' garden. The men took it in through the french doors and then very neatly and quickly put the fence back – Mrs Michael watching them like a hawk. The unloading went on, all the sunny afternoon. Linden Grove stayed quiet as it had been when they arrived. The comfortable old red brick houses dozed in the sunshine. A few people passed, mostly mothers with young children. A couple of dogs trotted. Cats came out to sit on steps or sniff the parked cars.

It was exactly the right kind of street. Nothing too posh or scary, but *nice*; a street where black and brown and white people lived together and nobody worried. Where people smiled as they walked by, where toddlers sat on the kerb and played with their toys; and on Sundays everyone would come out with buckets and suds to clean their friendly, shabby cars. No one was cleaning a car this afternoon, but a young couple, man and a woman, were doing some work on theirs, with tools laid out on the pavement. Diesel could hear them chatting to each other in happy, easy-going voices.

She sat on the front wall of number 57 (which had a little garden inside it, rather than rubble and rubbish) feeling as if she'd landed on a new planet. The big horrible barracks of their block of flats was the spaceship that had carried them from earth. Those rooms with no outside world belonging to them, nothing but a blank corridor and a lift that smelled of disinfectant (on its good days), had been their cabins. That balcony where you couldn't do *anything* except hang washing, because it was only about ten centimetres wide – that had been their porthole window on the emptiness of outer space. The journey had lasted years, but it was over now. They were safe on the other shore.

She felt like singing, as if she was five years old again: my wall! my door! my garden! my house . . . !

When the removal men had left she stopped being useless and idle, hung up Herbie on one of the coathooks in the hall – so he wouldn't get mislaid – and helped Mum and Dad to start putting things together: spreading rugs, arranging furniture, making beds, unpacking pots and pans. They even laid the stair carpet (downstairs was rugs, upstairs nearly-new fitted carpet left behind by the previous owners). As Mum said, it was the single biggest thing you could do to make a house *sound* normal. By the time they'd finished this feat, it was ten o'clock and they were starving. Diesel's mum heated up some tinned soup. They drank it from mugs, half asleep, and Diesel went off to have a shower and go to bed.

It had been a long day, a day taken out of normal life. Tomorrow Mum and Dad would be back at work and she'd be back in school. Linden Grove would carry on its quiet hours without them until evening, and then they'd come home. Home! Soon, day by day, living here wouldn't be strange and wonderful. Diesel felt that they should have done more celebrating tonight, because by tomorrow living in the new house would have begun to be ordinary. But never mind, they could have a housewarming party. Her mum and dad were great at throwing parties. There were plenty of things she wanted to decide about her new room, but they'd wait. She sat Herbie on the pillow, got into bed and closed her eyes.

Someone was playing the TV or the radio very loud.

It wasn't Mum and Dad downstairs. It was right by her ear.

She sat up. The loud music was coming through the wall from number 55.

So Mrs Michael was right, it wasn't an empty house. Unless it was an empty house haunted by pop music. She lay down again, thinking, *it's late, they'll soon switch it off . . .*

An hour later, by the luminous figures on Diesel's alarm clock, the music was still going on.

It was the radio, not a TV or a music centre. She became sure that there was no one actually listening, in the room on the other side of her bedroom wall. The radio-world voices were talking into a blank silence through there; and playing their loud music unheeded – like a tap left on with water pouring out of it in an empty bathroom. Someone had fallen asleep, forgetting to turn off the radio. The walls of the spaceship flats had been thin as cardboard. That was one of the things her parents had hated most about living there. You heard loud music, loud canned laughter from the TV, you heard people quarrelling, and slapping their children. It was miserable sometimes. But at least their neighbours at the flats had never been noisy all through the night.

She wondered what kind of bedroom it was, on the other side of her wall. How would it be furnished? With an old supermarket trolley and pieces of motor bike?

There was a whole succession of different presenters, as the hours went by. They all had the same kind of laid-back, soothing late night voices. Other people who were up all night for some reason phoned in, and chatted and laughed as if the radio presenters were their old and dear friends. It never stopped, loud and clear, right through 'til morning.

Diesel came down next morning heavy-eyed, feeling terribly sleepy, and with her brain not in gear. Mum and Dad were in the kitchen, looking miserable. She knew they had been kept awake too. Their bedroom wasn't right next to the guilty bedroom, but the noise had been too loud for anyone in number 57 to escape from it. She'd heard them getting up once. They had come onto the landing and she'd heard them arguing about whether they should go and try to sleep on the couch downstairs. But she'd been too sleepy and sort of hypnotised to call out to them, and in the end they'd just gone back to bed.

'It was a random incident,' Diesel's mum was saying. 'I'm sure it won't happen again.'

Dad's expression was grim. 'I'm not. I've got a bad feeling about this.'

'I bet Mum's right,' said Diesel. 'We couldn't be that unlucky.'

She understood why her dad was upset. It was only one night, but it was a bad omen, a cruel thing to happen just when their dream had come true.

When she came home after school she found Mum had cheered up. They went on arranging furniture – though it was only temporary, because they were going to redecorate. It was fun finding things that had got lost in the unpacking, and deciding where everything was going to go. Dad arrived back from work and they all kept on sorting and shifting, shouting answers to the quiz questions on early evening TV as they went from room to room; and eating sausage sandwiches (sausages fried by Dad, once he'd recovered the frying pan from the bathroom cupboard). But Diesel caught Mum and Dad looking at each other worriedly, and she knew they were thinking about the radio problem. It was important, because the move to this house had been such a treasured fantasy. They'd been looking forward to this wonderful change for years. Nothing, nothing was supposed to go wrong.

'Just look at the state of that place,' she heard her dad muttering to her mum, once. 'Just think about it. It's a dump, like no other house on the street; that tells the whole story. I could kick myself for not asking the estate agent. I'm sure he said it was empty—'

'Don't worry Leo,' said Mum, 'It was probably an accident. It won't happen again.'

About nine o'clock a car pulled up noisily outside their front door. They heard laughter and loud young voices. Doors slammed. The voices went into number 55. Almost immediately loud pop music started to play, drowning the Pragers' TV. Dad jumped up, grabbed the remote control and turned the volume as high as it would go. All that did was inflict a double torture of blaring noise. Mum and Diesel didn't say anything, there was no need. After a few minutes he turned the TV right off and sat glowering miserably in silence.

'Leo,' said Mum, 'I think you're over-reacting. They're noisy and we'll get used to it, like we did at the flats. They're not doing us any harm. It's a crumpled rose leaf.'

That was something Diesel's gran, Mum's Mum, liked to say. She'd say, *your life is like a bed of pretty roses girl, why are you complaining about one crumpled leaf?* The idea was

9

that a bed of roses would be perfect. Diesel always wondered about that; it sounded very uncomfortable to her. 'Huh,' said Dad. 'Seems to me more like real trouble.'

That night the radio coming through the bedroom wall stopped about 3 a.m. Then it started up again, louder than ever, half an hour later.

The next afternoon when Diesel came home Mum was already in, having been on an earlier shift at the DIY superstore where she worked. She was out on the front steps, taking old varnish off the front door with a heat gun and a scraper, and talking to a young woman Diesel recognised as one of the people who had been working on the engine of the green Peugeot 306, up the street, the day the Pragers had moved in. Diesel stayed and joined in the conversation. The woman was called Melanie, she was a trainee teacher, she had tousled dark hair, a silver nose stud and a cheerful grin. Melanie and her partner lived in number 53. He was a railway man, working shifts, so he was often around during the day. Number 55 was a corner house. There was a side street between it and number 53, so they weren't much bothered by their noisy neighbours. 'But I'm glad Adrian's home at unexpected times,' confided Melanie. 'It's a good job he's there to keep an eye on things, with the Knight brothers living next door. Not that they've ever *done* anything, except for the noise, but everybody knows about those boys. They are a problem.'

In the end Mum took a break from her scraping, Melanie came in for a cup of coffee: and gave them the full low-down on the people at number 55 . . . the problem family of Linden Grove. It was a sad story, said Melanie. She knew it all, because she had always lived on Linden Grove. Her mum and dad still lived further down the street. The

Knights at number 55 had been nice people, until the father walked out. But then the mother's new boyfriend had moved in, and the boys didn't like him. They quarreled with him violently, they started playing truant from school. Then the eldest, only fourteen at the time, had been caught joyriding by the police. He'd always been mad keen on cars. Both the older boys were. It had been something Jason Knight had shared with his dad, who was a wonderful mechanic: but after his dad had left and the boyfriend moved in, he'd got in with a bad crowd, and this was the result. Jason had been too young to be in serious trouble for a first offence, but his mum's boyfriend had given the boy a real beating, when the police brought him home.

'After that,' said Melanie, 'things started to go seriously downhill. The fights got worse, it never stopped. The boys' mother started drinking heavily. The house started to look neglected and awful, the way you see it now. The boys were never in school, always just hanging around. Eventually the mother's boyfriend moved to a place of his own, but by then it didn't make any difference.'

That was the way things had been for the last three years. The mother was usually off staying at her boyfriend's flat. Or else you'd see her being brought home to number 55 in an ambulance after some spree, her face all cuts and bruises. The house looked like a dump. Jason was seventeen now, he had left school with no exams and had never had a job; and the two younger boys were running wild. Martin, the middle boy, was maybe already following his brother's criminal footsteps. John, the youngest, was only twelve, but he was no better. He'd give you a mouthful of abuse if you so much as looked at him the wrong way.

Mrs Knight (when you could get any sense out of her)

said her oldest boy made his living fixing cars, work he got on a word-of-mouth basis – and it was true there were usually a couple of strange motors outside the house. But he'd been seen down in the town, by people who knew what they were talking about, with really bad characters: and though he'd never been arrested again, the police had been round questioning him more than once. Maybe it wasn't his fault, maybe he'd been working on the stolen vehicles without knowing where they came from . . . but there's no smoke without fire. And there were other rumours. A lot of people were convinced that Jason had been responsible for a series of burglaries in the neighbourhood, over recent months. Melanie thought it might well be true.

'I really think it wouldn't be fair not to warn you,' finished Melanie. 'Jason Knight is a wrong'un, his friends are worse, and I'm afraid poor Martin's going the same way. It's a shame.' She hesitated, looking a little guilty. 'I don't want you to think I believe all the gossip. I'll say this for them: they stick by each other, those three. The house is a tip, and the boys never look exactly smart, but they're clean and fed at least: and believe me, that's no thanks to their mother. If you say a word to her about the way her children behave – the loud music, the late-night noise, the strange cars coming around at all hours, she'll scream and swear at you. But she never does a blind thing to see them right.'

When Dad came home, Mum and Diesel told him what they'd learned. He took it badly. Mum unfortunately said something – half joking – about Diesel's bedroom window, which was an old sash window and not very secure. Dad immediately insisted on going out into the garden, to assess the chances of them getting burgled by their noisy neighbours. While the three of them stood staring at the back of the house, Michael from 59 appeared, and was soon confirming everything Melanie had said about the Knight boys.

'I didn't want to upset you,' he announced, with gloomy relish, 'but it's true. That Jason is a right young villain. *We're* all right, because of our Topsy. But if I were you I'd get some barbed wire round that drainpipe of yours. It'd be nothing to the Knight boys to do your house over. Over the wall, up the drainpipe, in through the bedroom window. The police are useless. I've tried to get them round. They won't do anything, won't even caution him.'

Topsy was Mrs Michael's terrier. She was an old, fat little thing, not much good for chasing burglars, Diesel thought. But she did have a loud bark.

Michael advised them not to confront the Knight boys over the noise nuisance. There was no point in trying to stop them playing their music, or slamming car doors, or talking loudly late at night. Other people had tried, he had tried it himself and got nothing but threats and swearing. The only thing to do was hope that the police would come to their senses soon: take Jason off to prison and have the other two put into some kind of Reform Home.

'Why didn't Mrs Michael or Michael tell us any of this *before*?' complained Mum, when Michael had gone back indoors, shaking his head sadly.

'People don't,' said Dad. 'They don't want to bear tales. Most people only want to tell you the bad news about *other* people, after you already know it.'

The three of them went indoors themselves, and sat around their kitchen table discussing the damage. Dad had horrible visions of securing the house with bars and locks, and broken glass on top of the garden wall. Like living in Fort Knox. Mum tried to comfort him and convince him that Michael had been exaggerating wildly, the way people love to exaggerate bad news. But it was still a horrible shock. Having really bad neighbours, Dad said, is one of the worst things than can happen to you, in terms of quality of life. And that was what they seemed to have found. Drunken mother, wild behaviour, criminals, violence, stolen cars, maybe stolen goods. The last two nights had been nothing, compared to what might happen. And there was no escape. The estate agent hadn't warned them, the neighbours hadn't warned them, they'd missed all the signs of trouble: now they were trapped, stuck here forever to be tortured – at the least – every single night by non-stop head-pounding pop music.

'You're jumping off the deep end, Leo,' protested Mum miserably.

But she seemed to be half-drowning in doom and gloom herself.

'Look on the bright side,' suggested Diesel. 'They haven't got a drum kit.'

Her parents didn't think this was funny at all.

Diesel felt terribly sorry for her mum and dad. They'd been looking forward to living in a house with a garden for so long, and everything seemed to have turned out right at last; and now this blow . . . It was as if they'd been given a new bike each for Christmas, and the very next day the wheels had fallen off, or something. But that night as she lay in bed, waiting for the radio voices to come through the wall, she felt almost disappointed when nothing happened. She hadn't totally minded being kept awake, not the first time anyway: not before she'd realised how upset her parents were going to be. It had been actually nice, lying there listening. Wondering about the room in which someone had fallen asleep, with the all-night station for an endless lullaby . . .

Walking to the school bus and walking home, she started thinking about the three brothers. How did it feel to be them? It must be horrible to have lost your dad, and have your mum turn into someone who didn't care. Diesel always felt completely safe and loved at home. But there were people at school who said horrible things about her because of the colour of her skin, so she knew how that felt. She knew how it felt to have people stare at you as if they were certain you were a criminal. It happened often, when she was out with her friends. They would be messing around, giggling, trying out the testers at a beauty counter maybe, and an assistant would come and see them off. But it was Diesel, the brown-skinned girl, who got the nastiest glares. It was Diesel they thought would be the thief.

Over the years she'd talked to mum and dad about this kind of thing, and they had talked to her. It always came down to *stand up for yourself but be patient, be forgiving, remember what Jesus said*. Diesel tried to feel that way, she wanted her parents to be proud of her. But she couldn't always be strong. Sometimes she felt like a worm, a crushed, miserable angry worm. She wanted to do something nasty – take a lipstick from the display, slap a girl who jeered at her for having crinkly hair, *just to show them*. So she wondered about the Knight brothers, Jason and Martin and John, without feeling as if they were enemies. What kind of life did they have? How did it feel to be called *bad*,

15

all the time; to stay off school, to live in a house with a heap of rubbish and rotting furniture outside?

On the fourth day of the new house, third time of coming home to it from school, she saw them for the first time. There was an orange sports car, an MGB, pulled up outside number 55, with the bonnet open. It was up on axle rests, with two legs in blue overall trousers sticking out from underneath. In the front yard there was a white kid with his dark hair cut bristle short, squatting on the ground messing with a mechanic's socket set, taking out the pieces and building them into little shiny chrome towers. That must be John, though he looked small for a twelve year old. Another boy was sitting in the rotten armchair, with his feet up over one of the arms, reading a superheroes comic. He looked about Diesel's age. He had the same pale skin and skinny build as the little boy, but his hair was rather long, with a limp fringe that flopped over his eyes; and which he kept shoving back. That must be Martin. The legs under the car must belong to the oldest Knight boy. The two boys in the front yard watched her while she stood fumbling for her new key, but they didn't look unfriendly. Diesel smiled at them. The young one ducked his head, like a shy animal. The one who must be Martin tossed back his overlong fringe and smiled in return.

She felt as if she'd betrayed her parents. But it had seemed the natural thing to do.

In fact smiling at the Knight boys turned out not to be a betrayal. Mum and Dad got over the shock, and pulled themselves together. They realised they had to take a positive attitude. The Pragers were Christians. They had to deal with their neighbours in a Christian way. That meant being tolerant and understanding, and making allowances for the tough time the family had had. As for the hair-raising stuff about Jason being a hardened criminal, maybe none of it was true. Just because he'd been in trouble with the police once, was no reason to believe he deserved such a bad name.

Nobody on the street had a good word to say about the Knight boys. Ever since Melanie had told her story, Diesel's mum had been meeting people who wanted to add their own tale: from the man at the off-licence on the corner of the main road, to the school-crossing lady at the junction. Even people at her work, who had heard she lived in Linden Grove, had come up to her, to tell her something bad about *those Knight brothers.* People are only human, said Diesel's mum. They love a good scare story. We shouldn't blame them too much, but we shouldn't believe their gossip either. We should treat our neighbours as if we know no evil of them. Because we don't. All we *know* is that three teenage boys have been a little inconsiderate. It's hardly a crime.

So Dad went round and knocked on the door of number 55, to have a word about the late night music and general noise. Diesel and Mum waited, almost holding their breath – trying to feel Christian (Diesel thought); but equally ready to phone the ambulance if Dad got beaten up, or if Jason Knight, hardened criminal, pulled a gun on him. Dad was gone about five minutes. He came back unharmed and looking almost ashamed of himself.

'What happened?' demanded Diesel. 'Who answered the door? What did they say?'

'Well, I had to knock like thunder, they've no bell, but Jason came to the door in the end. I spoke to him. He said

17

he was very sorry. He said number 57 has been empty for months. They'd got used to not having to worry about noise, and they didn't think.'

'Well, now we'll see what happens,' said Mum.

What happened was that that the music downstairs was still as loud, but it stopped at eleven o'clock sharp. The cars in the night pulled up just as noisily, but doors did not get slammed and nobody stood around in the street shouting and laughing any more. The radio in the bedroom next to Diesel still played, but it was never loud enough to disturb her parents. Mum and Dad cheered up. The three of them started decorating. The dream was alive again, and everything seemed to be okay. Whenever Diesel walked by, if Martin and John were in their front yard (and they usually were) they smiled at her and she smiled back.

She began to look forward to Martin's smile.

In church on Sunday, she stood among her parents' friends and her parents' friends' children, everyone dressed in their Sunday best, and offered a silent prayer of thanksgiving. Although she believed in God and was happy to go to church, Diesel usually used the time for daydreaming, and only woke up for the singing, which was the part she really enjoyed. But this, she felt, was a special occasion, so she said her prayer and made it a good one. The prayer then turned into a long thought, not quite a daydream but a long, interested thought, about Martin Knight. What did he do with himself all day, if he didn't go to school? Didn't he get bored hanging around doing nothing? Did he have a girlfriend? And was he ever going to speak to her, or would they carry on smiling, nothing more, for the next ten years . . . ?

She went home alone because her mum and dad had

church business. There was another, different car up on axle supports outside number 55 with the same pair of legs sticking out from under it. John was crouched on the kerb, his hands black with engine oil, a smear of the same black on cheek, passing bits from the socket set to his big brother (at least, Diesel supposed it must be big brother Jason under there). Maybe that's a stolen car, thought Diesel, with a prickle of unease running down her spine. She sympathised with the Knight brothers, but she couldn't help feeling *slightly* uncomfortable about the grown-up one. She wished he wasn't around all the time.

Martin was sitting on the wall of the grungey front yard, not doing anything much.

'Hi, neighbour,' he said.

It was the first time he'd spoken to her.

'Hi,' said Diesel, fumbling for her new key.

'You should put it on your key ring.'

'I know. I keep meaning to.'

She was embarrassed because she was all dressed up for Sunday, and Martin and John obviously never did any such thing. He swung around to face her, drawing up his knees. He was wearing a very battered pair of blue jeans and a T-shirt with the sleeves torn out of it, that was clean but creased and grey with wear.

'What's your name?'

'Diesel . . .' She felt her face go hot. 'It's Giselle, really. Like in the ballet. But I'm—'

'You're more of a Diesel,' agreed Martin, without her having to finish.

A remark like that would usually have embarrassed her no end. Diesel had long legs and a good figure, but she knew she didn't look like a ballerina. Everything about her except her legs was built chunky and on the square; like an engine. But from Martin, the comment sounded nice. After all, she knew Martin *liked* engines . . .

It would have been totally false to ask what *his* name was, but she couldn't think of any polite way to say that she already knew. (And you're Martin, Linden Grove's second most famous juvenile offender. You probably go burgling and you almost certainly steal cars, like your brother . . .). So she blushed more, mumbled 'see you' – and went indoors. But it was a start. She felt as excited as if something really important had happened, excited and a little bit scared. That night she listened to the soft murmur of the all night radio through her wall for a long time, smiling to herself, before she fell asleep.

Diesel and her mum and dad didn't see Mrs Knight herself for about three weeks after they moved in. Then one evening Diesel was doing her homework in the back room downstairs, surrounded by living room furniture; while mum and dad were painting woodwork and watching TV in the living room. It was about 9 p.m. Diesel heard the rumble of a diesel-engine, a black cab taxi engine, in the street. This was unusual for Linden Grove. People used minicabs to bring the supermarket shopping home and things like that, but taxis didn't roll up in the evenings. Then someone started hammering on the door of 55, the door without a doorbell. She stopped work and listened. The door was opened. Immediately there were raised voices, one of them a woman's, hard and slurred. The door was slammed. The raised voices went on. In the front room in Diesel's house either Mum or Dad climbed down the ladder, and turned up the TV.

They tried to mind their own business, that night. But they didn't get a chance. You couldn't make out many of the words, or understand what it was about, but you couldn't help hearing a furious quarrel, that went on and on. Once or twice they heard what sounded like the crack of an open-handed slap, once it sounded as if someone had fallen or been pushed downstairs: and John started to cry. After Diesel went to bed, it got worse not better. Downstairs Mrs Knight went on yelling at her oldest son; and he was giving back as good as he got. Things were crashing about as if someone was throwing pans at the kitchen walls. Upstairs, through the wall beside Diesel's head, there was no music, just the sound of John loudly sobbing. She'd worked out that Martin and John must share the bedroom where the radio played. Tonight she recognised Martin's voice – talking softly, trying to get the kid to calm down. But poor John just cried and cried. Diesel pulled her pillow over her head, feeling ashamed that she had to eavesdrop on their misery. She must have fallen asleep like that. She woke up half-suffocated, from a dream in which she was searching for Martin, in a house that had jagged broken glass for walls, and rusty supermarket trolleys for furniture.

Diesel had gone back to sleep after her pillow-on-the-head dream woke her. When she woke again there was rain battering against her window, but through the rain she could hear another sound that seemed to have migrated from her dream. It was a Saturday morning, she didn't have to get up for school. But she got up and went and looked out of her window. Rain was pouring down, and the wind was tossing the branches of the overgrown trees in the garden next door. But the three brothers were out there, bare headed and without their coats. They were sitting on a broken-down sofa which stood half hidden in long weedy grass, three dark-haired boys graduated in size like the Three Bears. The biggest one – it must be Jason – had his arm round John, hugging the twelve year old and rocking him as if he was a baby. Martin, next to them, was hunched forward over something that lay on the ground. He seemed to be systematically smashing something made of glass, with a half brick. She couldn't see his face, but she could see how fiercely he concentrated on grinding whatever it was to powder. Then he looked up, straight at her bedroom window. Diesel stepped back, feeling ashamed. She didn't understand what they were doing out there, it must be something to do with the row last night: but she could see how miserable they were.

Later that day she went into town, to meet her two best schoolfriends. She had nothing particular to do in town, but now they lived in Linden Grove the town centre was walking distance away. She and her mates, Anita and Bev, never tired of wandering round the two new indoor malls in the pedestrian precinct, Chapterhouse and Sanctuary: window shopping and chatting. Diesel's mum and dad didn't really approve. They felt that Diesel and her friends ought to be *doing something* in their spare time, not just vaguely hanging about. But they didn't mind, so long as they knew who Diesel was with and when she would be home. She'd never seen Martin anywhere but at number 55, never passed him in the street or seen him hanging out with other teenagers. But there he was, sitting on the rim of the fountain that was called The Elephant, in Chapterhouse Square, the open plaza between the malls. There was a concrete elephant with a castle on its back standing in the middle of the pool. The water spouted out of its upraised trunk. It was a memorial for an ancient pub – old enough to have been locally famous – called The Elephant and Castle, that had used to stand on this spot. The rain had stopped, and the sun had begun to come out. He was smiling at her.

'Hi,' said Diesel, coming over to him. She sat down, hoping he wouldn't think she was being pushy. They'd never had much of a conversation yet, but they'd been saying *hello* for a while now.

'Hi neighbour.' He tossed back his fringe. His eyes had dark circles under them, and his face was so white the freckles on his nose stood out like tiny bruises. 'Um . . . our Jason said, if I saw you or your mum and dad, I was to say sorry for all the noise last night.'

'That's okay.'

'Mum will leave again soon,' he said. His face was set in a wry smile, he was trying not to look embarrassed. 'She never stays long, these days. Then we'll have some peace.'

Diesel looked at her shoes. They were nice shoes: sporty but with lots of style. She'd bought them a couple of weeks before, after long drooling over them in a shop window. The sight of Martin's broken-down trainers, beside them, made her unhappy. She wanted to explain that she'd had to save up for ages. But she knew it wasn't money that made the difference between them. Everyone said the Knight boys had plenty of money, even if it came from suspicious sources. It was the feeling of being loved, and cared for. She suddenly felt that she couldn't leave him sitting there alone, and there was no use in being embarrassed. He knew she knew all about his sad story.

'What were you smashing up,' she asked, 'in the garden this morning?'

Martin had his head down. He was staring – like Diesel – at their two pairs of feet.

'A gin bottle.' He looked up, and met her eyes, smiling a smile that looked both hopeless and brave. 'She'd thrown us out.'

'What, in the rain?'

'She does that. She comes home drunk, she yells and screams and tells us we're evil and puts us out in the back garden. What can you do? Jason can't hit her, she's our mum. We know he'd protect us if he could, but he can't. So we let her shove us out, and sit there, and tell John-boy everything's going to be all right.'

'I'm really sorry.'

'It's not your fault. She wasn't always like this. It's like, Dad went away and so did she. The Mum we used to have went away and never came back . . . Are you doing anything right now, Diesel?'

'I'm meeting friends.'

'What if you tell them you've had a better offer, and come with me instead?'

Diesel was glad Martin didn't expect her to stand up her friends, with no explanation. She wasn't that sort of person, and it made her feel happy to know that Martin understood that. She went to find Anita and Bev, at the cafe where they usually met (they often didn't have the price of three coffees between them, but it was more sophisticated than meeting outside a shop). She told them she was doing something else, and came back to the Elephant Fountain. She was almost expecting him to have gone, but Martin was still there.

'Okay,' she said, trying to sound completely casual. 'What's the better offer?'

'Come on.'

So she walked with Martin Knight to the bus station, wondering what on earth had come over her. She had never done anything so bold before in her life. Her heart was thumping and she had that strange fluttering feeling inside that people call having butterflies in your stomach. To make things worse, she couldn't think of a single thing to say to him. They walked along in complete silence, and then stood and waited for a bus in silence. Maybe Martin was having the same problem. Or maybe he did strange things like this all the time, or maybe it was a joke, or maybe . . .

The bus they took was a country bus, one of the green and yellow single decker kind. Martin told the driver they wanted to go to a village called Browclough. They each paid their own fares. Diesel was almost surprised that he paid his fare, and spoke to the driver politely. It wasn't the sort of behaviour you expected from one of the dreaded Knight brothers. She knew she shouldn't think like that, but gossip rubs off, even when you don't want to believe it. That's why telling nasty stories about people is so wrong, she thought . . . It was even harder trying to think of something to say, having let such ideas into her head. He'd let her have the window. She sat beside him, without uttering a word, wondering what was going to happen. The streets went by and turned to fields, the road was lined with blossoming hedgerows. Soon the fields began to merge into slopes of moorland hills. I must be mad, thought Diesel. Where is he taking me? And are we going to go through this whole afternoon, in total silence?

She turned to him, steeling herself for the effort. 'Where are we going?'

Martin shrugged, and smiled. 'You'll see. A place I like.'

They got off the bus in the middle of Browclough. Martin stared at the timetable on the bus-stop pole, with a frown of concentration. 'Got to make sure you get back in good time. Okay, let's go. It's about a mile. You don't mind walking?'

'No, I like walking.'

They walked through the poky little moorland village, tongue-tied. Diesel had stopped feeling embarrassed, but it was still a big problem to know what to say. They'd hardly said a word to each other before. She'd smiled and he'd smiled. They'd said 'hello', and 'hi', and 'see you later'. But as for conversation the most personal thing he'd ever said to her, the *only* personal thing he'd ever said to her before today, was *You're more of a Diesel*. It wasn't enough to form a basis for easy chat. She walked along, swallowing those butterflies that were trying to climb up her throat, and wondering if Martin knew that she liked him. Not as a neighbour, not as a poor boy from a broken home, but as . . . the boy with the floppy dark fringe and twinkling brown eyes, a boy she liked to think about. He must know. There was no way he'd have asked her to come with him like this, if he didn't know. But maybe he didn't. Maybe she was being stupid.

At last she steeled herself again and asked, 'Had you been planning this?'

'Not exactly. Yes and no. I'd been thinking I'd like to show you this place. I show it to people I like. Then I saw you there, and I thought why not now? It's through here.'

There was a stile by a gate in the blossoming hedge. They climbed over it; and there was a footpath leading away across the fields. It wasn't well trodden. There was a very

26

old battered sign reading *Cordeliers Abbey (ruined) ½ mile*. I must be mad, thought Diesel again, as the silence between them closed up once more, merging with the bigger silence of the empty countryside. He's taking me off into the middle of nowhere. There wasn't another living person to be seen. Little bursts of birdsong started up boldly and quickly ended – as if the birds were embarrassed and tongue-tied too.

The path took a turn into a fold of the hills, and there was Cordeliers Abbey. It stood in a green valley, under the slopes of the high moorland. There was no one in sight, only the ruins. Roofless walls of grey-gold stone stood up tall into the blue air, slender windows and smooth pillars flying high. Dark doorways lurked under notched keystone arches. Other walls hunched smaller, reduced to long naked lumps of hard core, all the squared outer stones vanished. Between the stones the grass was a short flowery turf. Big trees grew along one side of the valley, making a boundary of bright young leaves.

'Wow, what a beautiful place.'

'It's good, isn't it.'

'But there's no one here!'

'Yeah, it's weird. There's never anyone here, never any tourists. It's like, everyone in the world has forgotten this place exists. I only found it because . . . well, there was a school hike I was on, and I had a row with the teacher, and I walked off by myself. Down off the moor, and I just fell over this place. The good thing is, you don't have to pay to get in.'

Where their footpath reached the ruins there was an old ticket booth standing beside it. Martin grabbed the top of the counter, swung himself easily up and jumped down

27

inside. 'That'll be nought pounds no pence, no concessions and no picnicking! Take your ticket and move along please!'

Diesel squinted at the faded placard on the outside of the wooden booth. 'It says *here*, two and sixpence for adults, sixpence for children under sixteen. I think sixpence is about the same as two and a half p.'

He laughed and jumped back over, back on to the path, took out a fivepence piece and laid it on the dusty counter. 'Okay, I'll pay up. I wouldn't want you to think I was cheap.'

They went on. In some places there were little old rusty signs half buried in the turf. Diesel got down and pulled aside the flowers so she could read what they said: Refectory . . . Chapterhouse . . . Kitchens . . . Dormitorium . . . In the monks' privies there were rows of stone slabs with worn holes that had been carved into them, the size and shape of monkly bottoms. In the kitchen there was a huge dark chimney that you could stand in. When you looked up you could see pigeons flying over the patch of sky above, and a creepy dark squirming high in the stone throat. 'Bats,' said Martin. 'If you're here at dusk, you see them flying out. It's great, like a vampire movie. Except they're no bigger than mice.'

She let him lead her from place to place, feeling that the abbey was something like Martin's private property and he had a right to take charge. She kept wanting to go and look at the most complete and biggest part of the ruins, with the impressive tall walls soaring up against the sky, but he seemed to be saving the best for last. They walked around all the rest of the site before they went near that bit. Finally they went in, passing through a quiet square of lawn, with a double border of long, low, hard-core hummocks, that was labelled *Cloisters*.

'This was the church,' said Diesel at once.

It was obvious once you were inside. She turned to face the huge empty window behind the raised place where the altar had been, and knew she was facing east. All Christian churches have their sanctuary, the holiest place, at the east end. In the mornings the sun would come in through that tracery of broken stone, in a blaze of glory. For a moment she forgot about Martin. Hundreds of years ago people had stood here, the way Diesel stood in church on Sunday. The place was huge. Everyone from miles around had probably come here, to worship with the monks. She tried to think of those people, long ago: some of them daydreaming, some praying; some of them just waiting for this daily chore to be over . . .

Maybe if she closed her eyes, she would hear them singing.

'Yeah,' said Martin. 'It's the church.'

She started to explore, at first not noticing anything wrong, and not noticing that Martin wasn't following her. The roof had disappeared, and there was nothing left of the pillars that had held it up but a double row of massive hard core stumps. In the space between these and the outer walls stood the remains of several big tombs. Soon she realised that there were more tombs under her feet: tombs everywhere. The floor of the nave, the main part of the church, was covered in gravestones, most of them almost blotted out by turf and moss and flowers. She tried to read some inscriptions, but even when she scratched away the turf it was no good. The lettering was not English. It must be Latin (she knew that was the language the monks would have used for holy things) . . . and this brought home how very *old* this place was. It was strange to be walking over long dead bodies, bodies that had turned to dust . . .

'Oh,' she murmured, standing up and rubbing her arms. 'It's cold in here.'

All the high windows were filled with cloudless blue sky. More blue sky looked down from over her head. But the towering walls seemed to create a shadow and a chill, almost like invisible darkness . . .

'Martin, I don't like this place. I mean, I love the ruins. I just don't like this part.'

'Oh, really?' It was only then that she noticed he hadn't moved from his spot by the archway that led to the cloister lawn. 'Funny you should say that.'

'Yeah, it's weird. An ancient church ought to feel good. At least, I don't know about you but it ought to feel good to me. I'm a Christian.'

'But it doesn't?'

'No, it feels . . .' She shrugged it off. 'I don't know, spooky. I suppose it must be the walls being so high, the feeling of being closed in, the sight of all these gravestones and tombs.'

'You don't know why, but you walked in here and felt weird . . . Yeah. That's the way I feel myself.' Martin looked pleased. 'Spooked. I didn't tell you, I wanted to see what you said. No one else I've brought here has felt like me. John doesn't know what I'm talking about. Jason says I'm imagining things. You must be imagining the same things. We must be on the same wavelength. Okay, let's get out of the creepy dump. I'll show you something really good, the best bit.'

This time he took her right across the site, to the place

where the big trees grew, two by two, in a long avenue with short smooth grass like a garden walk between them. There was a fence on the further side of this avenue, and a field with cows in it.

'They're lime trees,' said Diesel.

'I didn't know that. Why are you grinning, what's funny?'

'Limes are called Lindens sometimes. This is a Linden Grove.'

The next moment she wished she hadn't said it. Martin's face shut down as if a door had closed. He lost his relaxed smile, and looked almost as bad as he had looked in the early morning, when she had seen him out in the back garden in the rain, smashing that gin bottle. She shouldn't have mentioned Linden Grove. She should have realised, Martin came here to forget all that.

'I'm sorry.'

He shrugged, and smiled his hopeless smile. 'For what? Now, shut your eyes.'

Diesel shut her eyes. 'Try and keep them shut. It doesn't matter if you can't, but I want to give you a surprise.' He took her arm and led her, slowly. She felt the sunlight and the shadow as they moved in and out of the shade of the great trees. There was a step, another, and a short drop into deeper coolness. 'Duck your head. More; bend right down, yeah, that's okay. Now be careful. But don't open your eyes, not yet.' The air was suddenly ice cold, and full of moisture. She could hear the sound of running water. She could feel, under her feet, that she wasn't walking on grass any more, but something harder and more lumpy.

'Sit. That's right. You're good at keeping your eyes shut. Better than my brothers.'

'Me, nerves of steel.'

'You can open them now.'

They were underground. They were in a big dark cave underground, with what seemed to be a river running through it. But it wasn't completely dark. In front of them stood a broad column of light. It rose, round and smooth as a pillar, until it disappeared somewhere above. The other end rested on moving water. Everything around this column lay in a shadow of light, visible but mysterious. She could see how wide the water was, and how swiftly it ran, and the stone walls like canal banks on either side; and the Christmas-pudding lumpiness of the earth walls above . . .

'Oh, wow! It's an underground river!'

'More like an underground canal. I think the monks must have built it. They must have diverted the river under here, long long ago. It's weird, isn't it?'

'You could find out. Wow, there's so much you could find out. The history of it all—'

Martin laughed. 'Yeah. I could look it up in the school library, couldn't I?'

Diesel winced. A Knight brother didn't do things like studying history books.

'I'm sorry. I keep saying the wrong thing.'

'I can read,' said Martin, staring at the dark water and that strange column of light. 'I can write and I can add up, and that's it. I hate school, so I don't go. I'm a hopeless case.'

'I didn't say that. I didn't say anything like that.'

'The teachers treat me like dirt, I hate them. Jason says I should *stick it out* but why should I? I'm not going to pass any exams. Why should I bother to turn up? No reason.

I'm done for, I'm worthless. The teachers know it, and so do I.'

The bitterness in his voice frightened her. It seemed to come from somewhere deep, deep down: giving her a glimpse of a Martin she could never know, who was lost in the dark where she could not reach him. She shivered, her skin suddenly pricking with that feeling people call *someone walking over my grave . . .*

'Hey, I'm not trying to interfere. I said I'm sorry.'

He nodded. They sat for a while in silence. Soon Diesel could have told him that she didn't like *this* place much, either. It wasn't like the church, not a beautiful supposedly holy place that felt strangely cold and bad. It was underground, dark and secret; and that light effect was weird as well as beautiful . . . It was natural she should be spooked. But that didn't quite explain the creepy feeling she had.

She didn't say anything. She didn't want to spoil anything else.

'The light comes from a well shaft outside the big kitchen,' he said at last. 'You can look down it, but you don't see anything. The canal empties into the river that runs through town. I've found the place where it comes out, it's just about a mile away. But you can't follow the channel from in here. There must have been some roof falls. You'd need caving stuff to explore it, either way from this cave. I'd like to do that some day, but it doesn't matter. I just like to come here, sit and listen to the water. It feels like you never have to do anything, face anything, ever again. I like feeling like that. Being down so far, you know there's no use trying . . . that's when I'm best off. Come on, though. Can't stay here now. Got to catch a bus.'

He stood up, reached down for her hand and pulled her

to her feet. They both looked – in that strange light, for a strange kind of still moment – at Diesel's hand and Martin's, clasped together. Hers was smooth and brown. Martin's hand was white, and thin. It felt full of bones, and had scuffed knuckles and black rimmed nails, from helping his brother fix those cars, she supposed . . . Then they both, at the same time, let go.

They returned up an earth walled passage, Diesel with her eyes open this time, and came out from under a stone arch into the lime tree avenue. Why me, she was thinking. Why did you choose me, and smile at me, and bring me here? Just because I moved in next door? She didn't say anything. They walked across the ruins back to the ticket booth and the footpath. The sun was warm but there were rain clouds in the sky again, big ones massing over the hills. They got back to the gate and the stile, having said nothing to each other since they left the cave; but this time Diesel had hardly noticed the silence. It wasn't silence any more, it was understanding: a happy, sad, easily breakable under-standing between them.

Martin leaned on the top of the stile, looking out into the empty lane.

'How about if I kissed you?'

'If you like,' said Diesel, standing next to him, also leaning on the gate.

'Don't want to unless *you* like.'

'I like.'

So he kissed her. Just once, and softly: no snogging. Then he stood back, shrugged his shoulders, and gave her that hopeless smile. Didn't say anything; nor did Diesel. They walked into the village and caught the bus, without another word.

When they got back to Linden Grove, it was evening. They'd started talking again by this time. They were discussing what kind of cars they would like to own. Diesel wanted the new Toyota 1600, because it looked so elegant. Martin wanted a Jensen Interceptor, and was trying to explain what was so wonderful about this ancient classic. Diesel just naturally turned with him when they got to the front of number 55.

Martin hammered on the door. It was Jason who opened it. He frowned when he saw Diesel. It was the first time she'd seen the oldest Knight brother face to face. He looked quite like Martin, but his eyes were cold and grey instead of bright and brown. She could see beyond him a scruffy, littered hallway. Everything looked neglected. There was no carpet on the floor, and in places the wallpaper was hanging in shreds. She tried hard not to stare.

'Has she gone?' asked Martin.

'She was off hours ago. She won't be back tonight. She's going out with *him*.'

'What's for our tea?' said Martin. 'How about ordering pizza?' He turned to Diesel. 'You could stay, have some pizza with us? If you like.'

Diesel could see that Jason wasn't pleased about this invitation. But she could not resist that hopeless smile in Martin's eyes. 'I'll have to tell them next door,' she said.

She went next door and told her mum and dad. She wasn't late and they hadn't been worrying, so it was okay to ask. They were a *little* worried when she said she'd been invited to eat her tea with the Knight boys; and Mum was put out because she'd already started cooking. However, they made up their minds to it quickly.

'We have to trust them, Chloe,' said her dad. 'We have to

treat them the way we'd treat any other neighbours, we can't be suspicious or standoffish. Those boys deserve a chance. Martin is Diesel's age. If they're going to be friends, that's a good thing.'

Mum gave Diesel a look, while Dad was making this nice little speech, which seemed to say *I hope I'm wrong about what you're getting into*. But she made no objection.

The pizza boxes arrived soon after she got back to number 55. There was a stack of them. Martin hadn't known what Diesel would like, so he'd made Jason order a selection. The Knights' living room was an indoor extension of the back and front yards – tatty furniture, a haphazard square of grit-impacted carpet on bare floorboards; some black, greasy motor parts laid out on a sheet of newspaper. But there were two TVs, one of them a huge flat-screen model, a couple of Playstations, a music centre; a towering collection of CDs. Just like people said: the Knight boys were completely uncared for, but they seemed to be flush with money. Diesel tried not to look as though she was staring at the expensive things, and wondering if they were stolen (which of course she was).

Martin went to the kitchen and brought back cans of cola, with beer for Jason; plus a bread knife, for carving pizza, that wasn't completely free of engine oil. The three of them, Martin and John and Diesel, settled on the sofa, among empty drink cans and grubby car magazines, and began to feast. The pizza was a great ice-breaker. Soon Martin was grinning happily, and Diesel had forgotten to feel uncomfortable. Even young John – who looked peaky and tense, as if he was still getting over the nights he had spent crying, while his Mum screamed at his big brother – cheered up.

Martin and John, having gorged themselves to a standstill, started playing frisbee with the ham and pineapple pizza – the one no one had wanted after Diesel had picked off the nice squashy lumps of cooked fruit. Soon Diesel was playing with them, leaping over the furniture, diving across the gritty carpet; and laughing just as crazily. Jason didn't seem to care what they did. He'd finished his share of pizza and was plugged into one of the Playstations, a can of beer at hand, taking no notice of their antics. Through the wall, in the living room of number 57, it must sound like a mad house in here. A harmless, happy madhouse, Diesel hoped. Because that was all it was: three people having a lot of silly fun.

When the pineapple-less pizza had come apart into shreds too small to be thrown, and they'd calmed down and were watching TV, Diesel caught Jason looking at her: giving her a sidelong, suspicious glare while pretending to be absorbed in his road race game. He doesn't like me, she thought. He doesn't want me round here. If the house was really full of stolen goods, she supposed that wasn't surprising. But she wasn't going to be put off.

She woke up the next morning from a dream about being with Martin. She couldn't remember what they had been doing, but whatever she couldn't remember felt very sweet and happy. She lay looking at the ceiling, listening for noises in the room through her bedroom wall. Now this is where he starts avoiding me, she thought. I'd better start avoiding him first.

But when she came back alone from church, he was there sitting on the wall. He smiled, and she went to sit next to him. They sat there for an hour, kicking their heels, talking a little bit about cars, and teasing John-boy who was trying to put an alarm clock back together. The youngest of the Knight brothers had decided, just to be different, that he didn't like cars. But he was like his brothers in that he couldn't resist machines, so he'd decided to be mad about clocks instead. 'He prefers them with big moving parts,' explained Martin. 'He took his digital watch to pieces the other day. He was well cross when he found out what was inside. Weren't you John? Nothing for him to play with at all. So now he's got no watch, and we've got no alarm clock. He likes nice cog wheels and things that go clunk and thump. You should get yourself a steam-powered clock engine, John-boy.'

'Or a grandfather clock,' said Diesel. 'They have plenty of insides, I'm sure.'

'We'll have to look out for one,' said Martin. 'Me and Jason, when we go thieving.' He grinned at Diesel, and then burst out laughing at the expression on her face. 'Hey, don't tell me no one's told you any stories about us.'

'People talk,' she said, staring ahead of her, not wanting to catch his eye. It would have been easy to laugh and make a joke of it: say something like, *a grandfather clock would be too heavy, you'd never get it home*, or *You'd better make sure the getaway car has plenty of room in the back*. But she didn't want to do that. 'I know what the gossip is. I wonder if it's true, that's all.'

'What if it is?'

'Well, I think it isn't. But . . . you may as well know how I feel. I'd hate it if anyone was to steal my things. Or drive my mum and dad's car away. That's how I know stealing's wrong. Not because it's against the law. Because of knowing how I would feel.' It was a real effort, but she turned to look at him. 'I know your brother Jason has been in trouble with the police. For all I know *you've* never done anything wrong. I'm not going to believe any different, unless you tell me. You, yourself.'

'What if I told you I *am* a thief?'

'It wouldn't make a difference to me liking you. But it would make a difference.'

Martin smiled his hopeless smile. He slipped down from the wall, and went indoors without another word. John-boy followed, giving Diesel a reproachful look before he disappeared: as if she'd revealed herself as one of the enemies, one of the people who did the Knight brothers down.

She was afraid this counted as a quarrel, and felt she had been stupid and self-righteous. She wished she had never spoken. But maybe the way he had answered her was more of a warning, a challenge to her that she had to accept him as he was. Next day, when Diesel walked through the Chapterhouse mall on her way home from school, Martin was in the plaza as usual, sitting on the rim of the Elephant Fountain. He was nearly always sitting there when she walked by; and she would stop and they would talk for a few minutes. She knew he was waiting for her, though they always behaved as if he casually happened to be there. He stood up, when she came over. They began to walk, without saying anything to each other; just walking, side by side.

They wandered through the two malls, staring in the shop windows, not talking much; keeping close enough that their hands and shoulders sometimes touched.

'I've got to get home,' said Diesel, at last. 'They worry if I'm late.'

'Come down by the river, first.'

A zigzagging flight of steps ran down from Chapter-house Mall to the waterside. They took the steps to the walkway and stood there at the railing, under the cherry trees that grew along the path. On the other side of the river rose the old part of the town, and the cathedral that crowned the hill. A cold, blustery little wind was blowing away the blossom. Diesel watched the scraps of pink petals sailing along the dark water.

'Are we going out with each other?' asked Martin. 'What d'you think? Is that it?'

'I dunno. I know I like you.'

'I like you too.'

They turned to face each other. Martin unclipped one of her butterfly clips, and stroked her hair, 'That's nice. It's so springy, your hair. It feels really alive.'

She tucked back the hair, and couldn't think of anything to say in answer. She just shrugged, and smiled at him.

'Maybe it's better not to like people,' said Martin. 'It's dumb to get involved. If you care about anyone, you get hurt.'

She guessed he was thinking of his mum, and maybe his dad too; and maybe other people that he had tried to like. But they didn't see *Martin*, they only saw the boy with the reputation, the boy it was a waste of time to know.

'I don't know about being *involved*. That sounds weird. I just like you.'

'You're a go-to-church on Sunday, knives-and-forks on the tablecloth girl. I'm a pizza-from-the-box sitting on the scummy old carpet boy.'

'They say opposites attract.'

'What about twocking? Is that as bad as stealing?'

'What is twocking? I've heard the word, but I'm not sure—'

'Taking without the owner's consent. It means joy-riding.'

'I never heard that the joyrider car gets taken back where it came from.'

'No,' said Martin. 'We never bother doing that.'

'You mean you do take cars? You've done that?'

'It's just a bit of fun.'

Diesel felt tears sting. She bit her lip, to hold them back. The bleak look on Martin's face when he said *it's just a bit of fun* hurt her worse than knowing he really was a thief.

'Close your eyes.'

'Why?'

'I want to kiss you.'

She closed them.

'Don't open your eyes,' said Martin, 'and it's like the world doesn't exist. Only you and me, and this.' He kissed her, very softly, just the way he had kissed her at the stile; and then stepped back. 'Okay, you can open them.'

He sighed, and held up the butterfly clip. 'What if I keep this?'

'If you want. I've got to go now.'

She left him standing there, holding the blue and silver butterfly clip cupped in his hand, looking down at it. When she got back home she ran straight up to her room, and stared at herself in her mirror. There were cherry blossom petals caught in her hair.

Mum called up the stairs. 'Diesel? Are you okay? What's the matter?'

'Nothing! I urgently needed a wee.'

She went to the bathroom, to make this story true, and

41

sat on the side of the bath. It wasn't until she felt two tears roll on to her cheeks that she knew she was crying. Tears fell onto her clasped hands. Why was she crying? Maybe it was because she knew her mum and dad thought she was too young to have any kind of boyfriend. If they found out she was falling for one of the Knight brothers they'd be horrified, you could bet on that. No matter how un-Christian it was to be prejudiced against someone with a bad reputation. But it wasn't because of her parents that Diesel was crying. It was something different, something inside that was telling her: this is no good, this is going nowhere.

I've got to stop this now, she thought. Now or never. I've got to stop seeing him, stop thinking about him, otherwise I'm going to be really, really miserable.

Next day he wasn't sitting by the fountain. For the next few days she didn't see him at all. At night she lay listening to the radio, as it played softly in the room on the other side of her bedroom wall, and imagined Martin lying listening too; falling asleep to that soothing radio-world murmur. It will be all right, she thought. We'll just be friends. It will be better than all right. I'll get him away from Jason's influence. He'll change. He'll start to be more like me. He'll go back to school, and get on with the teachers. He'll stop taking cars, he'll work for his exams. He'll become the same kind of person as me, and everything will be all right.

But she knew it wasn't going to happen. She couldn't bear to give him up, or tell him to leave her alone, and yet *it was no good*. It wasn't the cars, it wasn't the playing truant. It was the emptiness that she sensed inside him, the darkness in him. Maybe Martin would make up her mind for her, and stop . . . whatever it was they'd both started. It wouldn't take much, he only had to stop smiling at her; stop hanging around waiting for her to pass by. Maybe that would be the best.

Another weekend passed. On Monday night, when she hadn't seen Martin for a week, Diesel was woken in the middle of the night by the sound of a car pulling up next door. She must have been sleeping very lightly, it wasn't one of those noisy, crashing pull-ups that Jason and his friends favoured. The first thing she noticed was that the radio wasn't playing in the room next door. Then she remembered it hadn't been playing when she went to sleep. She sat up, switched on her bedside light and listened, listened . . . wondering why she felt so frightened. She heard someone banging on that door with no doorbell, and she couldn't bear it any longer. She got up quietly and went downstairs, pulled back the front room curtain and peered out. The car that had stopped was a police car. It stood there with its lights flashing. A figure in a peaked cap stood at the door of number 55.

'Oh no,' whispered Diesel.

There was a drumming in her ears. She knew something had happened to Martin. Martin was in trouble . . . Having failed to get an answer from number 55, the policeman came and rang at the door of number 57. Diesel couldn't move. She heard her mother hurrying downstairs, dad coming after. She heard the policeman's voice, but couldn't make out the words, he was speaking so quietly. She forced herself to go out into the hall.

'Diesel,' said her mother, 'what are you doing up?'

'I heard the police car.'

Mum and Dad stood there, silhouetted against the

flashing police car lights. Another policeman appeared, behind the one on the doorstep. He had John-boy with him. John was small for his age, and the way he behaved made him seem like a little boy, even though he was twelve. He looked very young and very lost now. He was in his pyjamas – that is, an old, baggy, Dennis the Menace tracksuit – with a blanket huddled round his shoulders. His feet were bare. Mum was taking him in, the policeman was talking to her and then talking to his radiophone.

'What's going on?' whispered Diesel to her dad.

Dad shook her head. 'Ssh. I'll tell you in a moment.'

The policeman's radio said *fzz crrk* . . . 'Thanks, Mrs Prager,' he said, to Diesel's mum. 'And Mr Prager. We'll call you as soon as we've managed to contact the mother.'

'Mum, what's *happening?*'

'There's been an accident,' said Mum, with her arm around John-boy. 'Jason has to go to the police station. John is going to stay with us.'

'What kind of an accident? Is it their mother?'

'No.' Mum's hair was all on end, her old red dressing gown knotted tightly round her waist. She looked down at John-boy. He was staring up at her, but as if he could see nothing. His eyes looked like two black holes in his pinched white face. 'We'll make you a hot drink,' she said. 'Do you like drinking chocolate?'

'No,' said John. 'I only like tea. With two sugars.'

'Leo, take John into the kitchen and make him some tea.'

'It's Martin,' she said, quietly, when Martin's little brother was out of hearing. 'Apparently he was driving a car that the police were chasing. There was an accident. Oh, that poor woman. They're trying to find her now, to tell her. Oh, poor woman.'

44

Diesel sat down on the bottom of the stairs. She felt all the blood draining from her face. 'Is he dead?'

'Yes. I'm sorry, Diesel. The car crashed. He went through the windscreen. He was killed instantly.'

Two

Jason came round to pick John-boy up early in the morning. Mrs Knight hadn't been at her boyfriend's, but she'd been traced by the police, and told, and taken to see Martin's body. Diesel and her mum and dad had still been up when the police car brought her back to Linden Grove, but John had been sleeping by then, so they hadn't disturbed him.

It was Diesel who answered the door. Mum was close behind. She went to get John, and took him next door to his mother, leaving Diesel standing there. It was about seven in the morning. Diesel was still in her pyjamas, though she had not been back to bed. There hadn't seemed any point. I'll have to have a shower and get dressed, she thought. The idea of getting ready for school seemed so strange, it loomed through her dizzy mind like a visit to another planet. She stared at Jason Knight. His face was very white, with lines like deep grooves around his mouth. His eyes were red. It was weird to think of him crying. You wouldn't think someone who dealt with stolen cars and had a reputation with the police, would have the same feelings as a normal person.

'What kind of car was it?' she asked, wondering why he

was still standing there. Why didn't he go back to number 55? 'Was it a Jensen Interceptor?'

'No. It was a silver Ford Cougar. Nice motor, if you like modern cars. Martin never did. Must've been the other kid picked it out.'

'Was the car all right?'

Why was she asking such mad, stupid questions? Why was she asking about the car? Because there was nothing she could bear to ask about Martin.

'Write off.'

People said Jason had looked out for his brothers, but if Martin had turned out a thief, Jason had to take some of the blame. If he'd cared, he wouldn't have let Martin follow in his footsteps. She wanted to go indoors, but she didn't know if she could move without falling over, she felt so strange.

'The police shouldn't have chased him,' muttered Jason, looking down at the doorstep. 'No, what's the point. He shouldn't have been in that car. I'm to blame. I'm the one that taught him to drive. I thought it would help, I thought it would give him something . . . I shouldn't have done it, he was too young. But I did not teach him how to nick cars. He found that out for himself. *I couldn't stop him*. He wasn't a bad kid, I swear he wasn't. It was just, he got all twisted up over Dad leaving, and he never had a chance to straighten out.'

Diesel realised that he'd started crying. He didn't try to hide it, maybe he didn't realise that tears were running down his face. She was thinking about that scruffy living room, full of the bright shiny probably stolen goods, and the cold hostile way Jason had looked at her the day Martin brought her home with him. She was thinking, *you're to blame*. But it must be terrible to have your brother die, no matter what. She had better say something kind.

'Why did he have to die?' she whispered.

Jason shrugged. 'He was the one that was driving. Without a seatbelt. Other kid's okay.' He wiped his eyes with his scuffed, mechanic's knuckles. 'Thanks for looking after John-boy.'

It wasn't Jason who didn't care. It was Diesel. All she could feel was that she was very tired and dazed, from having been awake all night. No tears, no nothing.

'That was my mum and dad,' she said. 'I didn't do anything.'

Throughout the next few days, and nights, Diesel and her mum and dad, once more, didn't have much chance of minding their own business. They knew everything miserable that went on next door. They heard Mrs Knight's loud, wild sobbing, and the way she kept screaming at Jason; telling him he was the one who had led his brother astray, that she wished he was dead instead of Martin. They heard poor John-boy pleading with her to leave Jason alone. It was terrible to hear people making a cruel grief worse for themselves. Diesel lay awake at nights, and listened to John-boy crying himself to sleep, instead of listening to the radio-world lullaby. She wondered what it felt like to be dead, and whether Martin had known he was going to die. Did it happen very suddenly, straight from being alive and scared to the smash, or did he have time to see that he was going to go through that windscreen? What had his last thoughts been? But she did not cry. Everything was distant, she didn't feel anything.

Eventually the police finished with the body and Martin could be buried. The Pragers all went to the funeral, Mum and Dad taking time off work and Diesel taking time off school. There was a requiem mass beforehand in the Catholic church. It was the first time Diesel had been to a funeral, and the first time she'd been inside a Catholic church. It was a big place, which made the tiny size of the funeral party more depressing. Martin's dad hadn't turned up. No one had turned up except Mrs Knight, Jason and John, the Pragers, and Melanie and Adrian, the young couple from number 53. Diesel stood and knelt and sat when everyone else did, and looked at the painted statues in niches, the candles and the white cloths, in the same distant daze that had been wrapped around her since that night. Mrs Knight, Martin's mum, was a small thin woman with a yellowish face. Diesel had never liked the look of her. She didn't look any nicer wearing a new black suit and a new black hat. She was crying the whole time. Diesel tried to feel sympathy, but nothing came.

When the service was over the funeral-director people carried the coffin out to the hearse. The Knights got into a black car behind, and the Pragers and Melanie and Adrian followed in their cars. It was a dull day, neither warm nor cold; the sky was hazy. The cemetery was a dreary flat field full of headstones. There wasn't a tree, there wasn't a single monument that was different from the others. Even the flowers on the graves looked tired and drab. The pale, polished wood coffin was carried to Martin's grave, a narrow slot in the middle of a row. The sides of the pit were shrouded in a sheet of grubby artificial turf that had obviously been used many times before. Two rough planks were laid along the sides, with two ropes looping across the hole, on which the coffin would be lowered. Diesel stood staring, watching all these details, thinking *my friend is dead and being buried.* It bothered her that she could not work out what this meant to her. Was Martin being dead like something sad you see on the news, and forget the next day? Or was it something that would matter to her forever?

Diesel's mum had her arm around Mrs Knight, who was sobbing uncontrollably. Diesel remembered the morning when she'd seen the three brothers huddled together in the jungle garden; when their mother had shoved them out into the rain . . . Jason and John were wearing dark suits that didn't fit them very well. Jason was holding John's hand. John said something: Jason nodded, and bent down and murmured in his little brother's ear. Diesel wondered, what were they talking about?

The coffin goes into the grave, and the priest shakes holy water over it. Then, if you want, you take a handful of earth and throw it in. Then everyone can go. Diesel did what everyone else did. But when it was time to go she didn't want to walk with her mum and dad and Mrs Knight. She stopped to look at the small heap of flowers that was waiting to be piled on Martin's grave when it was finished. Though there were so few, there were still more flowers than people. There was a wreath from his mum, and one from Jason and John, and one from the Pragers. One from his father and one from his school, and one from Your Loving Nan, that must be his grandmother. They were all made of the kind of flowers that must be specially grown for funeral wreaths: dreary chrysanthemums and fake-looking carnations.

She looked up, and found Jason and John standing there, both staring at her so fiercely that it was as if they were trying to send her a telepathic message. Afraid they thought she was being nosy, she straightened and hurried to join her parents.

The brothers didn't come up to her, or say a word to her. They went off with their mother, and everyone else went home too.

Diesel didn't go into school that afternoon. It was too late, there would have been no point. She sat in the front room, doing nothing. Dad had gone back to work. Mum had taken the whole day off, but she was round at number 55. Mrs Knight didn't seem to have anyone else to look after her, and she could do nothing but cry. I'll hate it if we have to be friends with her, thought Diesel. I hope she goes away again soon. Dusk came on. Diesel sat there vacantly, not switching on the TV, forgetting to turn on the lights. Suddenly her mum, who must have come in without her hearing anything, was kneeling in front of her, where she sat on the sofa.

'Diesel? What's the matter sweetheart? Are you all right?'

'I'm all right. What time is it?'

She was amazed at how the hours had passed. It seemed like no time at all since she'd been in the cemetery, tossing a handful of dry, grey earth onto Martin's coffin.

'It's the shock,' said Dad's voice. 'Having someone you know die violently, it's a shock, even if it's not someone close. I don't think we should have let her go to the funeral.'

'I think I'll go to bed early,' said Diesel.

'But you haven't had anything to eat!'

'I'm not hungry.'

She went upstairs and washed her face and brushed her teeth, but she couldn't make the effort to undress. Days had passed, she had been trying to behave normally; but the funeral had brought it all back. She still didn't understand how she felt about Martin dying. Hardly anything had happened between them, so why feel so terrible? Dad must be right. It must be shock, a kind of illness. If it got any worse, she would go to the doctor and get some medicine. She switched off the light and curled up on the bed, fully dressed, with the side of her face pressed against the wall.

Listening for the radio.

She had been sitting like that for a while, when she heard something strike the glass of her bedroom window. She thought it must have started to rain, and that was just a noisy raindrop. But the sharp, single rap came again, and again. She got up – she'd been in the same position so long that her legs were stiff when she tried to move them – and went to look out. Two white splotches of faces looked up at her, from the garden of number 55. She opened the window.

'Diesel,' hissed John's voice. 'Come down! We want to talk to you.'

She was dressed so she just went down, and quietly let herself out of the back door. She had never climbed over the wall to investigate that wild garden, the way she'd planned when they thought the house next door was empty: but it still looked easy. She scrambled up on top, then slithered and dropped into the jungle full of old furniture, the lair of the supermarket trolley and the motor bike parts. The brothers were sitting on the old sofa.

'What is it?' she whispered.

'Come here. Sit down, we want to ask you something.'

There were lights inside the Knights' house. Diesel could see a figure moving, silhouetted through the curtains of a downstairs window. 'Don't worry,' said John. 'She won't come out.'

'Don't tell me she threw you out, tonight.'

'No. But she won't come looking for us. She's too drunk,' explained John-boy simply.

Diesel came over slowly – feeling uneasy, even in her grief, about Jason being there. But she sat down, perching herself on the arm of the rotting sofa.

'It's about Martin,' said Jason. 'We're going to shift him.'

'*What?*'

'We're going to move him,' said John-boy. 'You saw that cemetery. It's horrible. We can't leave our Martin in that dead-people farm. An' *her boyfriend* is going to pay for the headstone. We can't let that happen to Martin. We've got to move him somewhere else.'

'What are you talking about?'

'We've got to move our Martin,' repeated John-boy patiently. 'To his own place.'

'We're going to bury him at the ruined abbey,' said Jason. 'It's where he'd want to be.'

'You can't do that!'

'Don't see why not. It won't be that hard,' said Jason. 'I can get a van, and a couple of lads to help, and they'll keep quiet. We'll do it at night. I watched the gravediggers, I know where to get all the stuff we'll need.'

'I think it's against the law. I'm *sure* it's against the law to dig up graves.'

'I'm not bothered. If we get caught, then we get caught. I'm not leaving him in that miserable dump, not without trying to get him out. He's my brother. I want him in a place he loved. He took you there, didn't he.'

'Yes.'

'That's why we're asking you. He didn't take many people there, only us and you.'

Diesel felt something hard and sharp rising in her throat. She had stood through the funeral and the burial, never once thinking of what was inside that coffin. Everything that she had ever been taught told her that Martin was gone. Martin was not there. It didn't matter to Martin at all, where the coffin was laid. For the first time since he had died, thoughts of God and heaven went through her mind. Martin was somewhere else, on his way to another and better world. That was what she was supposed to believe; she was sure it was what she believed. But suddenly she couldn't help thinking of *what was inside the coffin.*

'Oh,' she whispered. 'Oh no, oh no . . .'

'Oh *yes*,' insisted John-boy. 'Oh yes. We can do it, and you've got to come.'

'That's not what she means,' said Jason, unexpectedly. 'We've made her think about Martin being . . . you know. Gone. Stick your head down on your knees, Diesel. You'll be better in a minute. It keeps hitting me too. One minute I'm normal, then I remember again.'

Jason was right. She felt better. She sat up, wiping her eyes with her fingers. 'I'll do it.'

When someone important to you dies, you have to do something important, or your grief will be stopped up inside and it will poison you. People in England used to wear black for a year. In some parts of the world people still tear their clothes and put ashes on their heads. Diesel and the two brothers would take Martin's coffin from the battery farm for dead people. The mean grave in the factory row in that miserable dump would be empty. The headstone that was going to be put up, paid for by his mother's hated boyfriend, would mark nothing. Martin would be lying under the flowery turf, in the shelter of the slopes of the moor; in the quiet ancient place he had loved.

When she finally got to bed that night, Diesel slept soundly for the first time since Martin had died. In the morning she woke up feeling horrified at what she had agreed to do. She knew it was breaking the law. When she thought about getting involved with something like that, and with Jason Knight's dodgy 'friends', she was very scared. But she was much more frightened just of the whole idea. Digging up a coffin, pulling it out of the earth . . . carrying it to the Abbey ruins at night. She couldn't believe that she'd said she would come along. She wanted to tell her parents, or even call the police, get someone to stop it happening. But she knew she couldn't. She couldn't tell tales: and however frightened she was, when she thought of that miserable, dreary field full of identical headstones, she felt worse.

In the end she decided she had to go through with it for John-boy's sake. She couldn't let him go along on his own, with Jason and Jason's criminal friends.

If it was going to be done it had to be done quickly, while the earth of the new grave was still disturbed and their further disturbance wouldn't show. Quickly was better for Diesel too, because she didn't want to have time for cowardly second thoughts. Two days later John told her that everything was set up. That night she let herself out of the front door, very quietly, after midnight when her parents were sound asleep. A dark panel-sided van was waiting at the corner of the street. There were three figures in the cab, three strangers' faces obscured in the darkness:

55

two of them white and one of them dark-skinned. Diesel didn't try to see them too clearly. She didn't want to know anything about them. Jason got out of the back and let her in. John-boy was there inside, white faced and huge-eyed, sitting on a heap of canvas sheeting. There was a coil of rope too, and some long handled spades; and three bulging heavy-duty bin bags.

The cemetery gates were locked up with a padlock and a chain, but that was no obstacle. One of Jason's friends got out and opened up the padlock as quickly as if he'd had a key. They drove through, and he shut the gates again so no one would see anything suspicious. But there wasn't much danger. The cemetery was on a quiet stretch of road, and there weren't going to be many passers-by at this hour. They parked the van as near as they could get to Martin's grave. Diesel was supposed to stay in the back with John-boy. But she was afraid that Jason and his friends would make a mess, or leave the flowers in a jumble. Mrs Knight was coming to the grave daily. She might notice something wrong: and then there would be trouble. So she got out. She didn't try to get John to stay behind. She wouldn't have liked to stay in the van by herself, in this darkness surrounded by graves; and he was only twelve. Together they carefully lifted the wreaths and laid them in order, well out of the way. Jason's friends spread the canvas sheet. All the earth that had to be dug up would be piled on that, then shovelled back. The digging began. Diesel and John-boy walked away, along the track. Though it was past midnight they could see fairly well. There was a big moon in a clear sky; and the lights of their home town made a glow all round the horizon. The rows and rows of headstones stood pathetically still, like people in a weary waiting room, or like a sad crowd waiting for a parade that never came by.

'I bet they all wish they could come too,' said John.

'I bet they do.'

'What d'you think being dead is like?'

'I don't know,' said Diesel.

'It couldn't be worse than being alive,' said John.

The digging didn't take too long. When the sound of shovelling stopped and the tackling and lifting of the coffin began, Diesel and John looked at each other, and walked further away. It was no use, they could still hear everything: the muttered orders, the grunts of effort, the heaving and hauling. Once there was the loud clang of a spade being dropped. They heard the back doors of the van being opened, and the bin bags being heaved out. Then something heavy and long grated on the metal floor; sliding inside.

'What's in the bags?' asked Diesel softly.

'Building rubbish,' said John. 'I mean rubble, like. They filled them out of a skip by a building site. D'you think that's wrong?'

'I don't think it matters.'

There was more shovelling. Then silence.

'Let's go back,' said John.

They met Jason coming to fetch them. His friends were lifting the canvas and piling the spades and rope into the van. Diesel appointed herself in charge of making sure everything at the grave was exactly as it had been before. Jason and John helped her with the flowers. Jason's friends stood by the van while this was going on, one of them smoking a cigarette; talking quietly but in ordinary voices – as if this was an ordinary night's work. When Diesel thought everything was okay, they turned the van's head-lights on to check. Jason walked around the grave, shining a big flashlight closely over the ground.

'Not a sign,' he said. 'Everything's the way it was. Let's get out of here.'

Diesel picked up a smouldering cigarette butt, squished it out and stuck it in her pocket.

Now there was a coffin with them in the back of the van. It was covered by the stiff folds of the canvas sheet. John and Diesel and Jason sat with their backs against the front seat, and the van started up. Soon they were through the gates, headlights switched on again, heading out of town. Diesel put her arm round John, and he got hold of her hand. It helped a bit, but Diesel felt completely sick and miserable. The idea of moving Martin to the peace of the abbey ruins didn't mean anything, now the grave-shifting was happening. She did not dare to think about *what was inside the coffin*. She had to think about having a difficult task and getting it done: a good deed, a favour for a friend. That's the first part over. Now the next.

A friend that she was never going to see again.

They reached the gate in the lane outside Browclough village. Everyone got out. Jason and two of his friends heaved the coffin over the gate, and then the spades and the canvas sheet and the rope. They waited while the friend who was doing the driving went to park the van somewhere off the road. Then the four young men (the three strangers were young, all about Jason's age) piled the spades and rope and canvas on top of the coffin; lifted and shouldered it and carried it along the flowery path, with Diesel and John following behind.

Out here in the country it was really dark, but the

moonlight made the darkness clear and strange, as if this wasn't night but another kind of day: in a different dimension, or deep under water. Diesel picked flowers – not choosing them but just pulling them from the long grass as she walked. She couldn't see the colours, only the difference between them: white was white, but gold and pink and green were shades of grey. The coffin-bearers stopped to rest, and went on. They came to the old ticket booth, and passed it. They were among the ruins.

We got him here, she thought. Another part of the task accomplished.

When she realised they were heading for the shell of the church she started to feel uneasy, but at first she could not remember why.

Jason and his friends carried the coffin in by the west end, where there was a big gap in the walls. One mouldering segment of a wide, richly carved archway survived, jutting into emptiness. They walked under it, laid the coffin down and stood looking around. Jason's flashlight playing along the length of the nave, over the standing tombs and the floor of turf and gravestones.

Diesel gave her flowers to John.

'Hold these.'

She went and joined the four men. She still tried not to look at the faces of the three she didn't know: she was sure it was better the less she knew about them. She nodded to them awkwardly, and spoke to Jason. 'Are you going to bury him in here?'

'Yeah. But we left the crowbar in the van. We'll have to fetch it.'

'What do you want a crowbar for?'

'To open one of the tombs.'

'You can't bury him in with someone else!'

Her voice came out loud and shrill, specially loud in this place. Jason's three friends stared at her, their shadowy faces shocked.

'Well, yeah, we can. We have to. That's the way it has to be.'

'You can't!'

'Look, give me a break. I've thought this out. We can't dig a new grave. We couldn't get it deep enough, and we'd never manage to leave no trace of the digging.'

'But no one comes here!'

'I'm not going to take the risk. In here is the best place. We're going to pull up one of the flat tombstones. I came here in daylight and gave it a bit of a try: it's not hard to shift one of them. We move a stone, we put him in, we put the stone back and there's no sign that anything's been moved. It's all sorted, just let us get on with it.'

Jason sounded angry, and she was frightened. But her fear was swamped by the memory, strong and vivid, of how Martin had felt about this part of the ruins.

'But you can't, you can't—'

He scowled at her. 'Leave it out. I brought you along because I know Martin would want you here. But *don't give me any bother*. I can't take it, not tonight.'

'He didn't like the church. Being in here gave him the creeps. Me too.'

Jason moved so suddenly and sharply she thought he was going to hit her. He only took her by the shoulders. He glanced at his three friends, who were watching this argument uneasily, and spoke in a fierce undertone. 'Stay out of this, okay? If you're spooked go outside. Take John-boy, and wait outside 'til I call you.'

'Martin would want to be in his cave,' she insisted, 'by the underground canal.'

She saw Jason's tense, dangerous expression, clear enough in the moonlight, get even more stressed. '*That* place. Yeah, I know where you mean. I'm not putting him in *there*. I hate that cave. I know that's where he used to go when he bunked off school. He used to go there and sit in the dark . . . He's sat down there, time after time, and got himself in the mood that would make him go out and twock a car, make him bunk off school forever, make him give up trying to survive. *He's not going down there.* Go and wait outside.'

She couldn't protest any longer.

John looked at her unhappily when she came back to him, he must have heard the argument: but he said nothing. He handed her the flowers, the bunched stems warm and sticky from his tight grip. They went and sat on one of the low, lumpy hard-core walls. An owl hooted. A breeze brought them the sweet scent from the lime avenue, where the trees were in flower. But the calm determination that had carried Diesel along, since she agreed to take part in this adventure, was shattered. She had lost her certainty that however strange and wrong and frightening this was, she was doing something that Martin would have wanted. Now there was just a long wait for something to be done that she knew should not be done.

She didn't say anything to John, and he didn't say anything to her.

At last Jason came to the gap in the west end wall and called them in.

The moon was right overhead now, and very bright. The ruined church was filled with a cold, silver glow that seemed like dead daylight. You could see a black line round every pillar and around the edges of all the carved stone in the soaring walls. The shadows between the tombs looked as if they'd been painted there in black ink. About half way down the nave, in front of a bay in the outer wall that must have held a side chapel, the three strangers were standing. They moved off, taking the spades and the crowbar, when Jason came up with Diesel and his brother. The flat tombstone that they had lifted was lying on the turf-covered paving; beside it there was a jet black rectangle. It didn't look like a hole in the ground. It looked like a chunk of solid darkness standing there. Then Jason shone his flashlight, and they could see Martin's coffin, lying down below them in the dark.

'There was nothing in there,' said Jason, as if he was trying to apologise to Diesel. 'Just an empty pit. It must be hundreds of years since this grave was used. Whoever was in it, they're dust long ago. So you see, he doesn't have to share.'

Diesel nodded. She knew this was wrong but she wasn't going to argue any more. She knelt, dropped her bunch of flowers into the hole, and stood up. The three of them, Jason and Diesel and John stood together, looking down. John got hold of Jason's hand.

Jason began to speak, in a low voice.

'What passing bells for them that die like cattle . . .'

After a couple of lines, Diesel realised that he was reciting a poem. It was about boys, and young men, dying pointlessly in war. Martin didn't die in a war, she thought. He wasn't a soldier. But the words seemed right for the cruel waste of Martin's life and death . . . She didn't feel anything much about being in the ruined church now. It didn't spook her. She only felt that this was a *dark* place, in spite of the brilliant moonlight. It was not a happy place, not a good place; and no matter if it had been a House of God, she was sure bad things had happened here. But Martin being dead was a bad thing too. Maybe his body *should* be here, not somewhere beautiful and peaceful. Leave him in the dark, she thought. It's right. He's dead and for no reason. Where else should he be?

'And each slow dusk a drawing down of blinds,' finished Jason. He turned to Diesel. 'It's about the only poem I know. I've always liked it. Written by someone called Wilfrid Owen, he was killed in the First World War.'

She was surprised that Jason Knight knew a poem at all, but not very interested. What did it matter? 'Yeah, Wilfrid Owen,' she said dully. 'We did war poetry at school.'

'I wanted to say something, do this properly. You go to church, don't you? Martin said you believe in it, all that. D'you want to say a prayer?'

She tried, and nothing would come. She shook her head. 'I can't.'

'Okay, don't worry. He *wasn't* a bad kid. Not deep down. He'd have pulled out of it, the twocking and all that. He would have been all right.'

'Yeah,' said Diesel, without conviction. Part of her wanted to shout at him, *it was your fault. You gave him a bad example!* But that would do no good.

She and John stood back. Jason's friends came up again. They put the slab back into place, carefully knocking the edges down into their old grooves with the end of the crowbar. And then, the same as at the cemetery, the flashlight check. As far as they could see, there was no sign that anything had been disturbed.

'I'll come back by daylight,' said Jason. 'To make sure.'

They returned to the van: Jason walking with his mates, Diesel and John following behind. Task accomplished, thought Diesel. All except getting home without being caught. On the drive, Jason's three friends talked a bit, but no one spoke in the back. Once they stopped at a traffic signal, and the lights from outside shone on the earth-stained spades; the folded canvas sheet. Diesel stared at them, shocked to realise what weird things she'd been doing, or helping to do; looked up and found John smiling at her sadly.

'Innit weird?' he whispered. 'I'm glad we done it, though.'

She nodded, and smiled back, tears stinging her eyes.

Now I know the answer, she thought. Martin was important. I will never forget him. And I am glad that I have done something to mark his passing. I have mourned him, I have laid him to rest. She wondered would she go on knowing Martin's brothers, or would they go back to being just those dodgy Knight boys next door? Somehow she knew that couldn't happen. She would always be bound to Jason and John, by the memory of this night.

But she didn't know, she couldn't guess, what this strange link would mean to her.

Her parents never knew she'd been out. They were fast asleep when she got home and let herself in, as dawn was breaking. She cried a lot, for the first time, when she went to bed that dawn; and it helped. Something inside her that had been sitting there hard and cold since Martin died, seemed broken and reformed by those tears. By the time a couple of days had passed she could hardly believe that she had been a grave robber. It was as if that night had been . . . not a dream, but something that had happened in another world, one that she would not visit again. Apart from the three strangers, who didn't count, no one knew except John and Jason – and she knew that they weren't going to talk about it. The deed that tied them together would be like a secret even from themselves. She was still sad, and still lay listening for Martin's radio late at night: but she was back to normal.

Mrs Knight stayed on at number 55. Diesel's mum was kind as kind to her. But it was very difficult. She had no job, nothing to distract her. She hardly went out, she let Diesel's mum do her shopping. All she did was sob and cry at the top of her voice, and yell at Jason and John. Diesel and her mum and dad knew all about it, of course. They couldn't help hearing everything, day and night.

Diesel found it hard to sympathise.

'I think you shouldn't let her get dependent on you,' she said to her mum. 'She's never nice to you, she just expects more and more.'

This was true. If Diesel's mum didn't go round every day, as soon as she got in from work, Mrs Knight would be on the doorstep of number 57, being horrible and whiney. Any suggestion that she might feel better if she started doing things for herself got a mouthful of tearful abuse and accusations.

'Well, I'm afraid that's how it works,' said Diesel's mum. 'If she was a lovely person with lots of friends, she wouldn't need us. It's because she's the way she is, and she's got no one, that we can't leave her to fend for herself.'

'Remember what Jesus said. It's *the poor* we have always

with us,' said Diesel's dad ruefully. 'The poor doesn't have to mean people with no money, it means any people with nothing of their own. No way round that.'

Diesel took comfort in the fact that she knew her dad shared her opinion of Mrs Knight, though he was as good a Christian as Mum. Diesel and Dad would be as kind as they could manage, but they were both secretly living for the day when Mrs Knight would go away and be horrible somewhere else . . . But she did listen to the things her mum said about not judging people; and about not blaming people when you don't know how you would behave if the same things happened to you. About caring for people who *need* care, and not expecting them to be angels . . . It made her think of Jason Knight, and feel guilty about the way she couldn't help blaming him for Martin's death. Whenever she got the chance she tried to smile and say hello.

Luckily, when she saw him, he was usually a pair of legs sticking out from under a car, so she didn't have to make much of an effort. She met John often, when she was on her own way home from school. Now that she was avoiding her old route home, through the Chapterhouse Mall, they came back from the bus the same way. He'd have a satchel over his shoulder, or he'd be carrying a folder of work: things she had never seen in his hands before. They'd talk, telling each other the gossip from their different schools and comparing teachers' crazy behaviour. John's mum had kept him at home after Martin died, because she couldn't bear to let him out of her sight, but apparently Jason had insisted John had to start going to school again.

They never mentioned Martin. The hurt was still too close. Neither of them wanted to break down and cry. But Diesel knew they were both thinking of him. She almost began to look forward to the day when they would be able to talk about him again, and laugh about things he'd said: about how he'd loved cars as if nice motors were the only reason for being alive; about how he used to tease . . . John said that he might soon be going to live with his gran for a while. Diesel felt that might not be a bad idea. It would get him away from his big brother's influence – and save him from hearing all those constant rows between Jason and his mother.

She didn't tell John this. She knew he wouldn't hear a word against Jason. But she made up her mind she would get the grandmother's address, and be careful to keep in touch.

At number 57 the decorating went on. Any time they could spare from school and work, Mum and Dad and Diesel spent on making their new house look wonderful. Mum made new curtains. Diesel put up some shelves in her bedroom, and varnished them herself. Dad improved the tufty lawn with regular mowing. The major decorating had to be done room by room, when they had time, moving all the furniture from one place to another as they worked; but none of them minded that. It was fun living among stepladders and dustsheets, and never having sit-down meals. Mrs Knight was far from being a perfect neighbour, but the worst of that was bound to be over soon, and the dream was still alive.

One Saturday morning, Diesel was on a ladder at the front of the house, rubbing down the paintwork on her mum and dad's bedroom windows. Their next big task was repainting the front of the house; a deep red colour for the bricks, cream for the woodwork.

'Diesel?'

She looked down and there was John.

'Come down. I need to talk to you.'

She stuck her sanding block in the back pocket of her overalls and hurried down to the pavement. 'Hi. What's up?'

'Can you come out to the ruins, today?'

They had talked about going to visit Martin's grave. But the scared tone of John's voice and the look on his face told her something was badly wrong.

'Someone's found out!' she gasped. 'What's happened?'

'We don't know. But Jason says you've got to come out there with us, this afternoon.'

Diesel left her dad and mum to carry on with the sanding. They didn't mind. She went out with Jason and John to Cordeliers abbey. They drove there in Jason's car, the orange MGB that was always around outside number 55, while other motors came and went. John got in the back. Diesel sat in the front. She kept wondering if she was riding in a stolen car; or at least a car that had been bought with stolen money. But of course she wasn't going to ask!

John had refused to tell her what was wrong, he said she had to see for herself. Jason didn't say anything much. They walked along the footpath, through the field that she had last seen by moonlight. It was a warm, sunny afternoon. The grass had grown long, the hawthorn flowers were over, the fragile briar roses were in bloom. It puzzled her that she felt nothing. No sad memories returned: she was only very worried about what would happen if the grave-shifting had been found out. Then they came to the old ticket booth.

And there was Martin, his dark hair flopping over his thin white face; jumping up, swinging himself easily over the dusty counter . . .

She saw him, clearly as if she'd suddenly been swept through time to that other Saturday, cooler than this one, sunny between showers. It was as if someone had stabbed her . . .

'What's the matter,' cried John. 'Diesel? *Diesel?*'

She had stopped dead. She was staring at the ticket booth. On the counter lay a fivepence piece, that nobody had disturbed; that nobody had touched since Martin . . .

She pulled herself together. 'It's nothing. I'm okay. I wish you'd tell me what's happened, why we have to be here.'

'I can't, Jason won't let me.'

'I want her to see for herself,' said Jason.

They went straight to the ruins of the church.

'I came back the next day, like I said I would,' Jason explained. 'Everything was fine. We'd done a good job of clearing up. There wasn't hardly a trace of what we'd done. I cleared away a few scuff marks, rearranged a few chunks of moss, that was it. But we came back again . . . I came back with our John, to visit him. And that time, I didn't like what I saw. Look. What do you make of it?'

They had reached the burial spot: half way down the nave, at the entrance to the ruined side-chapel. Everything seemed different in the sunlight, but Diesel saw at once what the problem was. The slab over the grave-pit where they'd put Martin's coffin was not sitting square in the old grooves. At one end, a corner of the stone lay out on the turf; at the other there was a matching corner of darkness.

Jason was watching her face.

'We didn't leave it like that,' said Diesel flatly.

'No,' said Jason. 'I didn't think we did. But I wanted a second opinion, like; and our John's a bit young to be a

69

reliable witness.' He brought out his flashlight from the daypack he was carrying. 'You can take a look. The coffin's still there.'

He shone the torch down into the dark gap. Diesel tried to look. It was hard to see anything, peering from sunlight into that narrow darkness: the flashlight beam didn't seem to extend very far. But she could make out a pale shape in the bottom of the dark pit.

She stood up, feeling sick: swallowed hard. 'So, what's going on?'

'Enemies,' said John. 'We've got enemies, people who don't like us. They've been messing with our Martin, trying to steal his coffin. They've found out what we did, and they've come and tried to get him.'

'It could be,' said Jason, 'the lads that helped us did it because they owed me favours. They could have talked. I'm not saying I don't have enemies. Or it could be someone with a sick sense of humour, having a laugh.'

'Maybe the stone shifted on its own,' suggested Diesel. 'There was a lot of rain last week. Maybe it was off balance from being lifted and put back, and the rain made it slip.'

'You haven't felt the weight of it,' said Jason. 'Did you ever look at what was on the slab?'

'What do you mean?'

'The . . . the carving on the slab.'

She stepped back and looked down. The stone was better preserved than some of the others that showed through the moss and turf on the old church floor. It had a border of zigzag lines. In the middle there was a worn carving of a lion's face, with curly tongues of mane all around it. Something like a twisted loop of rope seemed to hang

70

from the lion's jaws. Beneath this there was a single short line of inscription, blurred by years and weather but still readable. NON LICET PERTURBARI.

'Do you know what it means?' asked Jason.

'I know what the carving is,' said Diesel. 'That's the Sanctuary knocker. In the cathedral, you know. In the olden days, I don't know how long ago, if you were a criminal, if you could get to that knocker and hang onto the ring, you couldn't be arrested. You had to stay in the precincts of the cathedral, and live there for a year and a day without committing any more crimes, and then you were free to make a new life. We did it in school.'

'I didn't know that,' said Jason. 'I've never been in the cathedral. But I meant the letters. Do you know what the words mean?'

'No, I don't. I've never learned Latin.'

'I found out. I looked up the words in a Latin dictionary in the reference library in town, and worked it out. It means something like, *do not disturb.*'

'Oh,' said Diesel; and for some reason the hairs on the back of her neck started trying to stand on end.

John giggled nervously. Jason shrugged. 'Well,' he said, 'Maybe you're right about the rain. That's all. Let's go.' But he was looking at Diesel in a significant way that she didn't like at all.

They headed back for the gap in the west wall. John ran ahead. Jason stayed with Diesel. She knew, with dread, that he was going to tell her something more, something worse. 'That was a good idea about the rain shifting the stone,' he said quietly. 'I'll tell him you've convinced me that was it. Poor kid: I've said too much to him. I forget he's only a kid. I'm a bit short of people to talk to, that's my problem. But

71

what I want to know is, would you come here at night? With me?'

She stared at him, a chill trembling rising in her throat. She had not known how terrible it would be to come here. She did not ever want to come near this place again. And however hard she tried not to judge him, she was suspicious of Jason Knight. 'What, alone?'

'Er, yeah. Don't worry. I'm harmless, honest.'

'But why? To help you catch your enemies? What use would it be having me here?'

'Enemies? Nah, there's no enemies of mine in this. That's what I made up for John's sake.' He shook his head. 'I can't explain. I want you to see something . . . if you can . . . that I have seen, here, at night. You won't believe me unless you see it yourself.'

In the strange, dazed state of mind she'd been in right after Martin's funeral, Diesel hadn't thought twice about sneaking out of the house at night. This time it was different. She felt terrible – on edge and guilty and scared – as she sneaked downstairs after midnight. Every step she took seemed to raise loud creaks from the floorboards. But her parents didn't stir, not even when the front door got away from her and shut behind her with a loud thump. Jason was waiting in the dark street, in the orange car.

They didn't talk much on the drive. Once she asked him, 'What is it we're going to see?'

'I'm not going to tell you,' said Jason. 'I don't want to put ideas in your head.' So she was left completely mystified.

It was four weeks since they had reburied Martin. The full moon had waned and vanished since then; and grown to the full again. It would have been as bright as on that other night, but there was a lot of cloud in the sky; and a breeze that kept blowing the clouds over the moon. Jason used his flashlight on the footpath, though this path felt so familiar now, Diesel thought she didn't need it.

'We don't want to be inside the church,' said Jason, 'I was in there the first time I saw . . . what I saw. Wouldn't fancy being so close again. We'll stake out that square lawn-place.'

'The Cloisters. Have you seen this whatever-it-is more than once, then?'

They were passing the ticket booth as she asked the question. She looked to see if the fivepence was there, but she couldn't see: there was too much shadow.

Jason sighed. 'I've been here every night since the day I came here with John and found the stone disturbed. First night, I really thought I'd catch some so-called friends of mine, mucking around. It was late, but I was out and about, not much peace at home. So I drove along out here, and walked to the ruins. That's when I saw what I saw.'

'I don't know why you think I can help. I don't know anything about your enemies.'

'I *told you*, this isn't about my "enemies". I've been back every night since. I've seen the same thing most times. Martin trusted you, Diesel, an' he didn't trust hardly *anyone*. That's why I've brought you. You're going to tell me if I'm crazy, or if . . . Well, you'll see. *Maybe* you'll see.'

Maybe it was because the night was darker, or maybe it was because of the company she was in, but when they left the path and stepped among the ruins, Diesel felt afraid of this place for the first time. It was a different feeling from

73

being spooked in the church, or from feeling watched down in the canal cave: but equally as unpleasant. Everything seemed spooky tonight. Every upright stone looked like a menacing, hooded figure. Ideas came into her mind, about the chanting ghosts of monks in dark robes gliding over the turf . . . But nothing stirred. They made their way to that square of green lawn, with the opening that led into the church.

'Now what do we do?' whispered Diesel.

'Wait, and watch.'

They sat on the stub end of a hard-core wall, where they could look up and down the nave of the ruined church without being seen from within. Every few minutes clouds covered the moon, and the silvery dead daylight was swept away by crowds of shadows; then the moon would sail into view again. Diesel thought about the three strangers who had helped to do the reburial. Were they the pranksters; and was she supposed to identify them? Was that why she was here? But what use would it be if Jason had a witness to his friends' mucking about? They couldn't exactly go to the police and make a complaint. *You see, officer, we dug up this corpse and went and buried it somewhere, and now we think someone else is trying to dig it up again*. She choked back a giggle. She must be getting hysterical, there was nothing funny going on . . .

'Are you going to move out of number 55?' she asked, to break the silence.

'Not likely. I'm not leaving John.'

'I thought he was going to live with your gran.'

'She's too old. And she lives in a tiny flat. No, I'm going to stick it out. John's promised me, as long as I stay at number 55, he'll go to school and he'll work and he'll behave himself. It's not so bad, as long as I keep out of her way as much as I can.' He sighed bitterly. 'I lost the battle with our Martin. I've got to make sure our John doesn't go the same way.'

Yeah, thought Diesel. Nice idea. Only maybe if you weren't there, with your dodgy friends and your dodgy activities, John would have a better chance.

But suddenly, Jason was on his feet. He gripped Diesel's arm, and pointed.

The moon was bare at that moment, the ruined church full of cold, pale light. Something was moving in there, down on the ground. It's a badger, thought Diesel. How silly. We're out here getting all scared, just to watch some wildlife . . . But the shambling form looked bigger than any badger. That must be an effect of the confusing moonlight, magnifying things. Yet there was something wrong. It was on all fours but not moving like an animal. *It was a human figure*, crawling on the ground.

'*What on earth?*' she whispered.

Jason's grip on her arm tightened. 'You see it?'

'I see *something*.'

'Well, that's one question answered,' he muttered.

The grey, moving thing wasn't coming any closer. Diesel leaned forward, trying to make out what it was doing. If it was a person, why was the person crawling on the ground? Did Jason's 'enemies' know about the stake-out? Were they trying to sneak up on the hidden watchers, like kids playing at Commandos or something? There was something very strange and creepy about the way that shadowy form moved . . .

'Do you know what's going on? Do you know who that is?'

'No and no. Wait.'

At last the figure got to its feet. It came up the nave, moving in a loose-limbed, shambling way as if it wasn't in complete control of its arms and legs. Diesel's mouth went dry. Her hair was trying to stand up again, and sweat had broken out on her face. She was sure it knew it was being watched. Its head moved around, as if it could smell or sense the intruders. *It was coming closer* . . . She wanted to run. But Jason was gripping her arm, and she didn't dare to struggle for fear of attracting its attention.

The thing came closer still. There was a sickly smell in the air. It must come from that thing. 'Oh,' breathed Diesel, 'it's *dead*!' What she saw, in the cold moonlight, was a dead body walking. She knew that, knew it *completely*, in every bone and nerve, and yet still she didn't believe it. The monstrous apparition came level with the cloister opening. Now it was standing no more than few metres away from them . . . Diesel would have screamed except that she was too shocked and horrified to make a sound. Suddenly, the moon vanished behind cloud and they were plunged in darkness. Diesel whimpered: too horrified to scream, too scared to run. Jason was trying to turn on his torch, with shaking fingers that wouldn't obey him. 'It's okay, it's okay,' he was babbling, 'stay still, don't yell, don't run, it won't go for us. This is what it does. It walks around the church, then it goes off somewhere else, don't know where, never followed it—'

The moon came back. The beam of Jason's flashlight died in that darkling, other-worldly light, and the ruined church was empty.

A few minutes later they were sitting in the car, in a layby down the road from the field path; the same place where the van had been parked the night they had brought Martin's coffin here. Diesel was thinking that at this moment, she loved the MGB so much she might as well be a Knight brother. It was modern and safe, and bright inside, and it had the power to take them *away* from . . . from that thing in the church, whatever it was.

'Do you think that was someone playing a trick on us?' asked Jason.

When the moon had shown the apparition gone Diesel had simply turned and legged it – not waiting to see if Jason came after her, not caring for anything but to get away. He'd caught up with her at the ticket booth, and they'd kept going until they got back to the car; the flashlight beam bouncing uselessly on grass and stones right underfoot, leaving the menacing darkness all around untouched.

'Is that what you think?'

'No,' he said grimly. 'I don't.'

'Then *what was it*?'

'I don't know. That's why I brought you here. You saw what I saw. You tell me.'

Diesel stared through the windscreen into the black night. She shook her head helplessly.

'Maybe we were hallucinating. Seeing things.'

'The first time . . . was very bad. I was in the church. I saw it clear. It came right up to me.'

'And then what? What did it do? What did it want?'

'I don't know. I ran. It didn't follow me.'

'But you went back again.' She was impressed, in spite of herself.

'Martin's my brother,' said Jason, as if this explained

everything. 'We took him and laid him to rest in there. But he's not at rest. Now what are we going to do?'

Diesel stared at him. 'What do you mean? That wasn't *Martin!*'

'You saw what I saw,' repeated Jason, looking at her hard.

'No!' cried Diesel. 'No! It wasn't Martin! Don't say that! That's impossible!'

Jason started up the car and they drove back to town. Diesel got into the house and into bed without disturbing her parents, but she didn't sleep well. She had some very bad dreams.

Three

The morning after this experience Diesel felt shattered. Half of her urgently wanted to talk to someone, tell her mum and dad all about it. The other half wanted to run away and hide, to wipe that apparition glimpsed by moonlight out of her memory, and never have anything to do with the Knight brothers ever again. Because she didn't want *anything or anyone ever* to remind her of what she'd imagined she saw . . .

But when she came back from school that day, slowed-down and heavy eyed from lack of sleep, she found another kind of crisis had begun. Jason was out at the front of 55, tinkering with the engine block from a dark blue Vauxhall that stood by the kerb with its bonnet up. He looked up and nodded at her shortly, but didn't speak to her, thank goodness. She shut the door of her own house behind her with relief. Then she heard voices in the kitchen. Mrs Knight was in there, talking to Mum. Diesel headed for the stairs, meaning to hide in her bedroom until the coast was clear, but someone called to her from the living room.

'Diesel!'

It was John, sitting on the Pragers' sofa like a lost parcel, if parcels can look terrified.

'What is it? What's happened?'

'My mum's moving back with her boyfriend. She says she's tried but she can't look after me, not in her state of stress. She's going to get me put in care. My dad doesn't want me, my gran says she's too old, and Mum says Jason is not a fit person, so I have to go into a Home.'

Diesel stared, shocked at the desperation in John's voice. 'She can't do that!'

'She's done it. She's told the social and they're going to come and take me away. Jason made her come and talk to your mum, but it won't do any good. She's made up her mind. And it's Jason too. He don't . . . he doesn't know how to act with those kind of people. They'll think he's no good.'

Diesel sat down next to him. She'd have liked to put her arm round his thin shoulders; but this wasn't an emergency like the night of moving Martin, and the kid had his pride. 'It won't happen like that, John. Your mum can't decide what happens to you, just like that. The social services will ask *you* what you want. Your *wishes and feelings will be taken into account*. We did it in Personal and Social Development.'

'I want to stay with our Jason,' said John, obviously biting back tears. 'An' that's what he wants too. But I won't be let.' Suddenly he looked much older than twelve, instead of younger. Like someone who is used to having things turn out for the worst, and expects nothing else. 'Nothing I want ever happens.'

'My mum'll help,' said Diesel. 'She always helps people.'

Strangely, this business left Diesel feeling more sympathetic towards Mrs Knight. You could see, in the weary and remorseful look in her eyes, and in the sad tone of her voice when she came to talk to Diesel's mum, that for once she was trying to do her best. It just didn't get through to her that John was terrified of being sent away from his brother, to live with strangers. In the end it worked out all right. Mrs Knight's efforts to get John taken into care did not succeed. Diesel's mum *did* help – mostly by calming Mrs Knight down, and getting her to see that poor John would be better off with as little disruption as possible in his life. Also – to the surprise of the gossips and rumour-mongers on Linden Grove – apparently Jason made a good impression on the social services people.

Mrs Knight moved out, after one last night of loud tears and bitter argument, and the situation at number 55 went back to much the way it had been before Martin died. Except that Mrs Knight was definitely not living there, instead of just being away half the time; and except that Jason and John would have a social worker keeping a close eye on them.

While the crisis was going on, Diesel had tried to put the thing she had seen out of her mind, and she had almost succeeded. But the day after Mrs Knight moved out, John caught up with her in town, when she was on her way back from school, and she could tell from the look in his eye that she wasn't going to like what he had to say.

'Diesel, Jason wants to talk to you.'

For the last few days she'd been able to take the common-sense view, in her head. But the part of her that was terribly afraid was much stronger than she had realised. She felt instantly sick . . . nearly the same blank, awful way she'd felt when she heard that Martin was dead. 'What's it about?' she asked. As if she didn't know.

'He won't tell me.'

She came with him, reluctantly, back to number 55, and followed him into the house. Indoors, number 55 was looking scruffy as ever, but very clean and tidy. Someone had vacuumed the hall carpet.

'You're getting to be good housekeepers.'

'Jason says we've got to be. You know we've got this lady from the social, Mrs Goodyear, checking up on us now. We have to show her all our bills and stuff, how we're *managing our budget*. It's daft. Jason has been doing that for years or it would never have *got* done. But we have to do everything they say, or the social will put me in a Home.'

Jason was in the garden, sitting on the rotten sofa, examining a weed-strimmer. He'd been cutting the grass, there were swathes of it lying fallen like a heap of dead green soldiers; but it seemed as if the strimmer had given up. Jason put it down, and looked bleakly at Diesel.

'Go in the house, John.'

'I won't,' said John. 'I know it's about our Martin. I want to hear.'

'Get indoors.'

'*No!*'

'Let him stay,' said Diesel. She was protecting herself. Jason wouldn't be able to say anything about the apparition while John was here. 'If it's about Martin, it's his business.'

'All right,' said Jason, with a scowl. 'I'm going to move him again.'

'But you can't!' exclaimed Diesel. 'You can't do that again!'

'What for?' demanded John, his face going whiter

than ever. 'Because somebody's been messing with the gravestone? If that's all it is, why don't you just find out who it is and sort 'em? Tell them to leave our Martin alone.'

'I'm not asking you,' said Jason, speaking to both of them. 'I'm telling you. I'm going to get my mates again, and do the whole thing in reverse. You're not coming along this time, either of you. I'm only telling you so you'll know, and so you'll know not to answer any questions, if anyone asks you. But they won't, because nothing's going to go wrong.'

'*Where are you going to put him?*' demanded John. 'He wants to be left alone!'

'I'm going to put him back in the cemetery of course.'

'You can't do that! You can't put our Martin back in the dead people farm! What good will that do? I'll . . . I'll tell Mum!'

'You do that,' said Jason, glaring at his little brother. 'You tell her. And I'll move out, an' you'll end up in a foster home. Your choice.'

John looked ready to burst into tears; spun around and rushed into the house.

Jason shrugged, started up the strimmer and began cutting the grass again, without looking at Diesel. Diesel went into the house. John wasn't in the downstairs rooms. Feeling as if she was trespassing, she climbed the stairs. There was no carpet on them, only battered slices of vinyl nailed onto the treads. Her footsteps echoed. She found John in the big bedroom, the room matching the one that belonged to Diesel's mum and dad. It looked as if it had recently been given a personality transplant. There were football posters and other boy-things on the walls, but the worn-down wallpaper was lilac coloured with little sprigs of flowers. The curtains at the window matched the wallpaper. John was lying on the big bed, not crying, just staring miserably at nothing.

'You used to sleep in the back room, didn't you?' she said. 'The one next to mine.'

'I used to share it with Martin. Jason let me move in here after Mum left. I hated sleeping in there after . . . I kept waking up in the morning and thinking he would be there, and he wasn't.'

Diesel sat on the end of the bed. 'Your brother can't go grave-robbing again. Someone will find out. We got away with it once, that won't happen twice. He'll get caught, he'll be in trouble with the police, and it'll be awful. We've got to stop him.'

'I know why he wants to do it,' said John. 'It's not "enemies". It's because of the ghost.'

She stared at him in shock.

'He *told* you about that?'

'He told me that he'd seen something, after the first time he went there at night. Then he went back to saying it must be some of his mates messing about, and pretended he'd been having me on . . . But I knew. He wouldn't have made a joke about something like that, and anyway, he was *really scared* that first time. I could tell. An' Jason doesn't scare easy.'

He sat up, and looked at her hard. 'I know Jason took you there, in the middle of the night. Did *you* see anything?'

Diesel wanted to say no. She wanted to say, *it was my imagination*. But the words stuck in her throat. 'I saw something . . . weird.'

John looked horrified. 'Oh no,' he whispered. 'Oh no. Then it's true. I knew, really, but I was hoping it might not be. But if you say it's true, it's true. Like Martin used to say, *Diesel would never tell a lie*. Oh no, what'll we do? What do you do for someone that's turned into a ghost? We can't leave him like that!'

'I said I saw *something*,' said Diesel, trying to think of Martin free and happy in heaven. 'I don't know what it was, but it couldn't have been Martin. Don't listen to your brother. Martin's safe, John. He's somewhere else. He's gone where nothing can hurt him.'

But in her mind the apparition rose, the memory made real again by the staring terror in John's eyes. She had tried to forget, but she could recall everything, with fearful clearness. The thing's sunken eyes. The slack-jointed, shambling way it had moved . . . Ghosts, if they happened at all, were supposed to be shadows, frail illusions. That monstrous thing, *a dead body walking*, challenged every-thing she had been taught to believe. About holy places, about the power of goodness. About death being a safe haven, a passage out of this world, beyond which there was only peace and God.

John was looking unconvinced by her reassurance. 'Then if it's not Martin it's some other creepy ghost, and that's equally as bad. It might go for our Martin. A ghost is dead, and Martin's dead,' he reasoned. 'One dead thing can hurt another. We can't leave him where there's some rotten ghost sneaking around. Jason is right, we have to get him out of there.'

'No! That's *stupid*.' Diesel was thinking hard. 'All right, suppose there's a ghost in the ruined abbey. I'm still convinced it will turn out to be some kind of hoax. I don't believe it, but suppose it's true. What if we find out the cause of the haunting?'

'What good would that do?'

'Maybe we could lay the ghost, if we know why it's there. Look, I'm getting an idea. Come back to the garden with me, I want to talk to your Jason again.'

Jason had given up cutting the grass. They found him in the living room, staring at daytime TV. The programme presenters (it was a cookery show) went on chattering in the background, while Diesel explained her idea.

'I'm going to do some research,' she said. 'I'm going to find out the history of the ruins. I don't believe it was, but if that was really a ghost we saw, there has to be a reason why it appears . . . Remember how Martin never liked the church? I felt the same. That place felt *bad* before any of this happened. I'm going to find out why.'

'Oh yeah?' said Jason, staring blankly at the TV. 'And what good will that do?'

'Maybe . . . maybe if we know why the ruined church is haunted, we can put it right. Maybe then the ghost will be able to rest.'

It was mad, but she found herself staring at the TV too. Someone was chopping up an aubergine, and sprinkling it with salt. *Now we leave this to drain, and that gets rid of the bitter juices*, said the TV cook. Jason didn't look round, but she could feel his scorn and resistance.

'Hey,' cried John, excitedly. 'I know! We could get the abbey exorcised! There *are* real exorcists, it's not just in horror movies. I've seen programmes about them on television. We wouldn't have to tell them about Martin.'

'That's a great idea,' said Jason sarcastically, still staring at the TV. 'Your exorcist would turn up, poke around, find a modern coffin in an ancient grave, and then we'd be in trouble.'

'My idea is better,' insisted Diesel. 'I'll try the Central Library, tomorrow.'

Jason finally turned and looked at her with those hard grey eyes. She looked back at him as boldly as she could, feeling as if she was protecting Martin, (thought it couldn't be true that Martin needed her help, not really).

'Go on then. Do your *research*. If it'll make you happy.' His hopeless expression reminded her of Martin.

'And meanwhile you won't do anything about moving him again? Okay?'

'Do your research,' said Jason, without smiling. 'And *then* I'll move him.'

Diesel went to the Central Library the next day after school. It was a new building, all glass and steel, with shiny lifts, open staircases and bright, sunny galleries. You could sit and talk, have a coffee; go online and find out everything that was happening in the modern world. Her heart sank as she climbed the curving staircase to the reference section. It was surely going to be impossible to find out anything about a ghost in here. Except on the fiction shelves, or in the horror videos. Any mention of a creature like that *dead body walking* would melt from the crisp, modern, pages of the reference books, wouldn't be able to hold its shape on a shiny computer screen. It would vanish, the way ghosts are supposed to vanish if you try to photograph them; the way a vampire's face doesn't show in a mirror.

She wasn't surprised, when she managed to get a place in front of a computer, that the local information network turned up nothing. The ruins at Browclough barely rated a mention in the list of sights to be seen. *No longer open to the public*, was all it said. So we were trespassing, thought Diesel. We had no right to be there. Not even that first day when he took me to see the place he loved . . . How typical of Martin, and Martin's life. She stared for a while at the glossy images, the banners and the buttons, that were happily inviting her to find out about canal rides and theme parks and four-star country hotels: and then gave up and went to the inquiry desk.

'I want to find out about a place called Cordeliers Abbey.'

'*What* sort of abbey?' asked the assistant behind the desk.

'It's a ruin. It's near here, but there doesn't seem to be anything about it on the local information network.'

'What did you want to find out?'

'Well, the history of it, what happened there, why it became a ruin. Anything, really.'

'Hmm. A ruined abbey . . . Strange, I've never heard that name. Is it a genuine ruin, or a nineteenth-century folly? You know, the Victorians were so fond of ruins that rich people used to build their own, to decorate their grounds. It was thought to be very romantic.'

'I'm sure it's genuine. It's near Browclough.'

'Then, let me see. You want to know why an abbey became a ruin. That could take us back to the Dissolution of the Monasteries—'

'Henry the Eighth. I know about that. Yes, it would be a place to start.'

'I'll see what I can find in the reserve stacks.'

Diesel filled out a form. It wasn't a very helpful form, because she didn't know a title to ask for, or a book

catalogue number. She was too embarrassed to put anything about ghosts. She put 'Cordeliers Abbey', then
crossed it out and put 'anything about old abbeys and
monasteries in this area' to be on the safe side. She didn't
know if the abbey had always been called 'Cordeliers'. The
librarian went away, and came back after quite a long time,
with an armful of big, shabby books.

'There you are. Have a look through these. I'm surprised
that the name is not familiar, I thought I knew all our local
history sites. I've brought you some history books. You
might find your abbey mentioned in one of them. Or in one
of these old memoirs about the area.'

Diesel found herself a place at one of the long, working
desks, between a young man who was making notes from a
science book full of equations, and an elderly lady who was
reading the tabloid papers. She began to check the index of
the first big history volume for the words 'Cordeliers', or
'Browclough'; or 'haunting'. The reference hall was full of
sunlight; and the buzz of quiet information-gathering.
Pages were being turned, screens being clicked, files being
consulted. *I'm not going to find anything*, she thought. But
the heavy, musty books themselves were like a link with the
past, with a world in which old legends were remembered
and ghosts could walk, so she started turning the pages in
hope and fear.

She found Cordeliers Abbey described in a book on the
sixteenth-century history of the Church (in Diesel's
county). What the historian had to say was very interesting,
almost shocking . . . It made her feel strange to read it, and
think of that peaceful place. She took quick notes. She now
had some idea, at least, why the ruins might have a bad
atmosphere. But there was no mention of a ghost.

The next volume in the pile had nothing to tell her, nor the next. Then she came to a book called *Witchcraft And High Magic In England*. She wondered why the librarian had given her this, when she'd asked about a ruined abbey. Had she somehow looked like someone looking for weird tales? There was no index. She started to turn the pages, reading bits and wishing she was doing this research for fun, or for school . . . The quiet of the library was soothing, and she fell into one of her church boring-bits daydreams. She was grown up, doing this work as part of her really great job. She was researching something for a TV show, and in a minute she would find it. She would fax the material back to her office, then she would go strolling down the shiny glass and steel stairs, to meet her boyfriend. She woke up, before she saw that boyfriend's face . . . to find herself staring down at a page where the word *Cordeliers* had snagged her eye and pulled her out of the dream.

She had found a ghost story about Cordeliers Abbey. Or rather, it wasn't exactly a *ghost* story, but it was exactly what she'd been looking for. She read, and as she read, her heart began to thump. She felt half terrified, half triumphant . . .

When she'd finished she shut the book abruptly, as if she was afraid the things she'd been reading about could escape. Her heart was thumping like mad now, and her mouth dry with panic. She searched furiously through the stack the librarian had given her. There was nothing else about *Cordeliers* in any of the indexes.

She dashed back to the desk. 'You've got to find me some more books! Something old, something really old and original about Cordeliers Abbey!'

'I'm afraid we don't have anything with that title,' said the librarian.

'But you have to have more. I need to know more! Are you sure you don't? Maybe you have something so old it didn't get entered in the computer catalogue. Let me look, on the reserve shelves. I really, *really* need to find out something.'

The librarian looked at her strangely. 'Well, this isn't a museum. We don't have any ancient texts, I'm afraid. Excuse me but I can't let you into the reserve rooms, and I can't let you see a book we don't have in the library. Are you feeling unwell?'

No, I'm not feeling unwell, thought Diesel. I'm going mad. I think I'm going mad. Her palms were sweating, she wiped them on her jeans.

If you knew! she thought, staring at the woman helplessly.

'We could try an interlibrary loan, if you can give me a title of a book to ask for. Are you sure you're all right? You look quite faint.'

'No,' said Diesel slowly, giving up hope. She turned away. 'No thanks . . . I'm fine, thanks.'

She went back to her place at the desk and searched again through her stack of dusty tomes. There was nothing more. The page flipping and scanning half-hypnotised her, so that she scarcely heard the ten minute bell. At the very last moment she jumped up, dug out some change, and copied the story which had given her such a shock of horror. She handed the books over the counter again and left.

When she got back to Linden Grove Jason was working on a white Toyota Celica; John was with him, handing him tools. The Vauxhall had gone. They were both smeared with engine oil. They looked almost happy – except for that empty space behind them, where Martin ought to be sitting lazily on the wall: offering advice, teasing his brothers, staring at the sky. She could almost see him there, head tipped back to keep his floppy fringe out of his eyes, looking at her with his hopeless smile . . .

'Well?' said Jason, startling her. 'Did you get anywhere with your *research?*'

His voice was sneering. 'Yes I did,' said Diesel defiantly. 'Do you want to hear about it?'

Jason shook his head. 'I know what I saw, and I know what I'm going to do.'

'*I* want to hear,' said John.

'Go on then. I can manage without you.'

John and Diesel went indoors, to the room where Diesel and the three brothers had shared a stack of pizza, one silly evening. 'All right,' she said, sitting down on one of the battered armchairs. 'Let's start at the beginning. Cordeliers Abbey was . . . Do you know about the Dissolution of the Monasteries?'

John shook his head.

'Well, Henry the Eighth decided to take over and be head of the Church in this country, instead of the Pope. He took all the lands and riches and buildings away from the monks and people, and closed a lot of abbeys and monasteries down. Some of them were good places, and the monks had been doing good things: looking after the poor and so on. But some of them were not good. Our Cordeliers was one of the not so good ones. The monks were a kind called *grey friars*. They were Franciscans, which means they were specially supposed to be giving up worldly possessions and spending their whole time doing good. But that wasn't what was going on at Cordeliers, not by the time Henry the Eighth was around. The friars were running a smuggling business. They used to murder anyone who got too close to their secrets, and dump them in that underground canal Martin found . . . Or that's what people used to say about them, anyway. So when the abbey was closed, the land given to someone else and the friars thrown out, nobody around here was crying for them. That's the first thing I found out. But the book said Cordeliers had *"an evil reputation"* before those days. That was how the friars managed to get away with their smuggling: people were scared to come near the place. So I went on looking.'

'And?'

She passed him the sheets of photocopy paper. 'Read that.'

'I can't,' said John, after looking at it. His face went pink. 'I can read, it's not that I can't *read*. But there's too many fs for s, and words I don't know.'

'Okay, I'll tell you, as best I can . . . About a hundred years or so before the Dissolution Of The Monasteries, there was an abbot at Cordeliers Abbey who was a magician. He was called Roger Monfort.'

'You mean real magic?'

'Of course I mean real magic. You wouldn't get a medieval abbot doing card tricks and pulling rabbits out of a top hat, would you?'

'But how could an abbot be a magician?'

'It was different in those days. What we call "magic" was looked on more as science, and Franciscans were supposed to be very learned, well up on all the secrets of nature . . . Only, Abbot Roger went a long way too far. At the time when he was abbot there was a war going on in England. It

93

was called the War of the Roses. It doesn't come into the story except that the abbot decided to hide the Abbey's treasure, for safety, until things calmed down. So he buried it in a secret place, with a magical guardian. This guardian was like a Frankenstein's monster: a sort of medieval zombie. To make it, the Abbot needed a dead body. It had to be the body of a criminal who had died by violence, but it wasn't too hard for him to get hold of one of those. There were lots of people being hanged in those days. He took the body from a gibbet. He used some powerful spells to make it into a monster with superhuman strength, and left the monster guarding the treasure. It was supposed to stay there, as if dead: but if anyone tried to take the treasure it would wake up and tear them to pieces. The thing was called 'The Boatman'. I don't know why. But 'The Boatman' started getting out of the place where the treasure was buried, and marauding around the country-side. It couldn't leave the abbey property, and it didn't attack the friars, but it would go into the neighbouring villages, which all belonged to the abbey in those days, and dig up new graves, and eat the dead bodies. If it couldn't find any dead bodies it would attack lonely travellers on the road across the abbey estate. Apparently that's the danger with this kind of zombie. If they go wrong they turn into ghouls, which means a creature that preys on human flesh. They prefer *dead* human flesh, but they're not all that fussy.'

John was gazing at her, round eyed. 'So what happened then?'

'Well, the monster was getting more and more out of control. So Abbot Roger repented. He decided he should undo his spells and rebury the zombie body on holy ground, in the church. The other friars knew Abbot Roger had hidden the treasure, and they knew that something evil was preying on the living and the dead in their neighbourhood, but they didn't know their own abbot was to blame. He hadn't told them about the zombie. He told them he would use his powers to banish the evil, and they believed him. He had them make a new grave in the floor of the church, and got a gravestone carved for it. When everything was ready he made them all stay out of the way, and fetched the monster – in daylight, when it was still fairly inactive, except when the treasure was under attack. He did all his spells in reverse, and reburied it.'

'Did it work?'

'That's the point. Apparently not. The man who wrote the story that I copied was writing three hundred years later. He says it was because of the bad zombie magic lingering on, like an infection, that the friars turned into evil smugglers, and he also says *many believe that the monster will walk again, unless it be returned to the place of the treasure it was set to guard.*" ' Diesel drew a deep breath. 'Then he describes what it looked like.' She read aloud from the photocopy paper, keeping her voice steady. ' *"A creature man high, with the limbs of very loose joints as if they would fall in flinders, the hide of a grey hue and the eyes sunken and filled with blood. It has the appearance and the stench of one long dead, but the grip of it is terrible, and its strength is foul and monstrous as its appetites."* Look, there's a picture.' She showed him the copy of the old woodcut that had illustrated this gruesome story. It was pretty horrible.

John stared at her. 'Is *this* what you saw, you and Jason?'

'If I didn't imagine it, I saw something like that.'

'Well,' said John shakily. 'At least it isn't Martin.'

'No,' said Diesel, firmly. 'Definitely not Martin. If we saw anything, what we saw was the abbot's guardian-thing. I'm sure of it.'

Then John's expression changed, from relief to horror. 'Oh no! Diesel! That means we've buried Martin in a place haunted by a ghoul that eats corpses!'

Diesel had been protected by the feeling of success. While she was explaining everything, she'd felt like the grown-up researcher that she'd been in her daydream in the library, proud of herself for getting hold of so much valuable information. John's face, blank and drained with shock, ripped through her defences. She heard the words she'd been saying. She saw the apparition again in her mind and felt sick, sick and terrified. The front door banged. Jason came into the room, in his greasy overalls. He looked from Diesel to John, with a scowl of exasperation, and stooped and picked up the piece of photocopy paper that had fallen from Diesel's hands.

'What's this?'

'It's what I found out,' whispered Diesel.

Jason stared at the paper, read it, crushed it furiously in his hands and threw it into a corner of the room. 'What's the point in that load of rubbish? You're scaring yourselves for no reason. I'm going to move him back to the cemetery. That's the end of it.'

'I want to go to the abbey again,' said John. 'He's my brother too. I want to be sure nothing's happened to him. I want to know Martin is okay.'

'Of course he's okay,' Jason said, in a gentler voice. 'He's dead. What could happen to him? You heard Diesel, before she went off on this daft *research* lark. There's no such thing as ghosts, we just imagined we saw something. I'll feel happier when we've moved him back to the cemetery, that's all. Now I'm going to clean up. You should be doing your homework. Send her off home and get on with it.' He didn't look at Diesel.

When Jason had gone John said, 'He's upset. He doesn't mean to be rude. He's been upset ever since he saw that thing.'

'I don't blame him,' said Diesel. But she was glad Jason was out of the room. She rubbed her arms. It was a warm evening, but her skin was cold as ice.

'So what do *you* think we can do?' asked John.

'I think we can lay the ghost,' said Diesel. 'If it "still walks" it's looking for the treasure. If we can find the treasure, and . . . I don't know, hand it over to its proper owners or something, the ghost would have no reason to haunt the abbey any more.' She sighed. 'The trouble is, the story I found doesn't give you any idea where to look. It's supposed to be taken from the wicked Abbot's secret confession of his evil magic, but it seems like he never confessed that bit. The book says Abbot Roger sealed up the hiding place, after he took the zombie guard away, and no one except him ever knew *where* the treasure was hidden.'

John frowned. 'If this was all hundreds and hundreds of years ago, then the treasure can't still be there. Abbot Roger must have dug it up, after the wars.'

'Maybe he didn't get the chance. Maybe he died before the Wars of the Roses ended.'

In the library, Diesel had been desperate because the story she'd found left out the location of the treasure. But she'd realised later that this was a *good* thing. It meant the secret had never been discovered. 'I think if the treasure had ever been found, there'd have been some mention of it in the books I read. There wasn't. I think there's a good chance it was never disturbed.'

'But you said Abbot Roger used all his powers to put the zombie out of action, and it didn't work. If a top medieval magician couldn't do it, what chance do *we* have? No, it's no good.' John sighed. 'You looked for information and you found some. But all you've done is prove that Jason is right. We have to get Martin out of there.'

'No! That would be crazy. You two are on . . . on probation, sort of. What do you think your social worker would say about grave-robbing? And there's no need to do it. Look, I don't really believe in this medieval zombie story, I'm desperately searching about for ways to stop your brother Jason getting you and him into trouble. But suppose it was *true,* it wouldn't make any difference. Because *that isn't Martin.* It's a wooden box with a dead body in it. If there *is* such a thing as a ghoul, if it *does* haunt the ruins by night, Martin can't be hurt by anything getting at . . . at what's in that box.'

Even to her own ears, it didn't sound convincing.

They went back to the ruins by daylight, the three of them together. John had persuaded Jason to take him, and insisted that Diesel had to come along. They left the orange MGB in the layby. Diesel tried not to feel frightened. Nothing was going to happen in broad daylight.

She was hoping, maybe they were all hoping, that this time they would realise the whole thing had been a mistake. When they looked at it again they'd see that the gravestone hadn't been moved. Diesel and Jason had seen nothing but a shadow in the moonlight, and the story in the book Diesel had found was a creepy story, nothing more.

It was very strange that the place was so quiet. On this hot, sunny summer Saturday, when the countryside around their town was bursting with people looking for things they could do outdoors, they were the only visitors taking the footpath to the Cordeliers Abbey ruins. She wondered why the place was 'no longer open to visitors'. Was it because no visitors had wanted to come here? It was as if the evil reputation of the Abbey had somehow stayed alive in people's minds, like an instinct, through hundreds of years. Something told the local people that this part of their past was best forgotten.

If only Martin had shared that instinct.

As they walked along the path, Diesel's thoughts went round and round. All right, suppose the Abbot's treasure had been dug up long ago; and the place was *still* haunted? Maybe they should try John's idea of getting hold of an exorcist. But how did you do that? Maybe she should ask her mum and dad. *Without mentioning anything about Martin*, she'd have to tell them she had seen a ghost, at a ruined abbey out in the countryside. She didn't know if they believed in ghosts. They ought to, because they were Christians and believed in spirits, and a ghost is a kind of spirit: but she wasn't sure. She tried to imagine how Mum would react, and how Dad would react. They wouldn't believe her. She would have to convince them that she was serious. Then she would have to convince them to help her. Really, she didn't know what she was going to do. Spells, exorcists . . . It all sounded completely mad, as mad and unreal as coming out here with the coffin that night, and much more frightening. But she would do it, do whatever must be done. *She would do something.*

She would not desert Martin when he needed her . . . If a dead person can need anything.

All this thinking and wondering and planning, it always came back to the fact that Martin was dead. She felt the sun, and saw the flowers: and Martin was dead.

The brothers had been walking on ahead. John dropped back until he was beside Diesel, and looked up into her face. Funny how she'd thought of him as a sullen, hostile little kid, much too young for his age. He was small, of course, but none of the rest of it was true. He just didn't give people his confidence easily. Like his brother Martin, he had learned not to trust the world to treat him fairly.

'Cheer up,' he said. 'I'm not worried. We're on the case. We'll sort it out.'

You aren't worried, she thought, because you didn't see that thing.

But she didn't want to say that.

'Come on, let's play stone football. It's Martin's game, he invented it.'

He found a stone to kick, and sent it flying. Diesel picked up the idea quickly, and to her surprise Jason joined in. Soon they were kicking along in turn, racing to be on the end of a pass and chipping it high in the air; John providing the commentary. Free kick to Prager, oh, a magnificent shot, oh, unlucky. The corner will be taken by Jason Knight, who passes to John Knight; the Knight brothers are cooking on gas this afternoon . . . The game went on, past the old ticket booth and into the ruins. John-boy was persistent, and very good at finding the special stone again, no matter how often it went into the deep grass. But perhaps Jason as well as Diesel was grateful for the distraction. It was a way to pretend, for as long as possible, that they had no serious, grisly reason to be here. The stone football went on flying to and fro over the flowery turf, scaring the sheep that had been let out to graze among the ruins, right up until they'd reached the west end of the ruined church.

John was the first of them to realise where he was.

'Hey, we're here!'

He darted forward, picked up the football stone and ran to the gap in the walls.

This is how it would be, thought Diesel, coming to a halt. If only everything was all right. We would be coming here to visit Martin's grave: a risky secret but a good secret. She stayed back, wiping her eyes, not wanting the brothers to see her crying. There were summer flowers in the close-cropped grass; but Diesel remembered the hawthorn blossom, the day that Martin had brought her here, in the springtime. How long ago that seemed. A sheep jumped up from behind a low wall and lolloped heavily away, startling her. There, she told herself. Nothing to be afraid of. It was probably a sheep that night, and those other times when Jason came here alone: a stupid sheep, looking strange in the dark . . .

Maybe all that was wrong was that Martin was dead.

She pulled herself together, looked up and saw Jason and John standing there; two figures both looking small against the blue space of the great broken arch in the west wall. They must be waiting for her.

They were standing very still . . .

Her heart jumped. She ran the last few metres, and stood with them, staring. At first she couldn't work out what was wrong. Then she realised that there was a black slash in the green floor of the ruin, like a mark or a stain of some kind. About half way up, alongside a place where there'd been a side chapel. A black slot in the ground.

Martin's grave was open.

Jason said, 'Diesel, you stay here with John. I'll check it out.'

'No!' howled John. 'He's my brother too!' He raced away from them, and Jason didn't managed to catch him. They were all together, when they came to the brink of the grave and saw what had happened. The slab had been moved, as if something had flung it aside. It was lying wrong side up on the ground. Martin's coffin was clearly visible in the bottom of the pit. But the lid had been pulled off, it was propped slantwise against the earth wall.

The coffin was empty.

'Oh, no,' wailed John. 'No, no!'

Diesel dropped to her knees at the edge of the pit, staring down.

'We should go to the police,' she announced, shakily. 'It's the only thing we can do. Someone must have found out about what we did. They've stolen the body as some kind of mean, vicious, nasty joke. We've got to go to the police and confess everything, and beg them to help us get Martin's body back.'

'The police won't help,' said Jason.

He was kneeling on the edge of the grave too, looking at it carefully.

'The police won't help,' repeated John-boy, furiously. 'The police are *useless*. They killed Martin. We've got to get him back ourselves. We've got to hire some muscle.'

'Don't talk like that,' said Jason. 'The police didn't do anything wrong.'

But he was looking at Diesel, and the tone of his voice was strange. She'd almost stopped feeling scared of Jason, since the night he'd brought her to the ruins. She'd been fighting him, over that stupid plan to move the coffin again, for his own good as well as for John's sake. But now he was staring at her so hard, he frightened her again . . . She saw that he was pointing, keeping his finger low so John couldn't see, to the wall of the pit. She saw something like a wet, sticky smear that glistened in the sunlight, but showed black where it trailed over the grass at the grave's edge.

What was that? A *hand print*?

She bent to have a closer look and immediately jerked back. Whatever it was, that smear of black, it smelled foul. She scrambled to her feet and backed off: she couldn't help it. The slab that had covered Martin's grave was lying beside it now, the inner face upwards. The inscription, under the image of the lion's head, was the same as on the outside. The carving, that had been hidden for hundreds of years, was fresh and clear.

NON LICET PERTURBARI.

This must not be disturbed.

'Let's get away from here,' said Jason. 'C'mon John-boy. There's nothing we can do. Let's go home. We'll get him back, our kid. We'll rescue our Martin, don't you worry.'

Diesel went to bed that night thinking about Jason and his enemies. Jason, who had friends who were villains, who fixed stolen cars, who was a criminal himself. He must have offended some very nasty people. They must be real monsters, to steal a corpse. She tried not to let the terrible alternative into her mind. Images of that dead thing with its loose, shambling limbs, picking up the big stone slab with monster strength and flinging it aside. Images of rending and tearing, horrible ideas. She lay listening for the radio, as she always did, although she knew she would never hear it again . . . and fell asleep.

She dreamed she was back in the ruined church. She was with John and Jason by the opened grave. The sun was bright and the sky was blue, but there was a blackness in the light and a bitter cold in the air, hidden under the sunshine. She was looking down at the empty coffin, and the coffin lid which had been thrust aside. Jason wanted her to see something else, but she kept looking at the coffin. The white satiny lining was fresh and unstained, although crumpled and dented where the body had lain. Coffin lids are nailed down. Someone had torn the lid away, wrenching the nails loose. She could see the points of the nails, sticking up out of the edges of the lid. Not twisted, not wrenched, still straight. As if, instead of someone hauling the lid off from above, something inside had pushed, violently, upwards.

'Look,' said Jason's voice. 'Look at the coffin lid.'

'I'm looking,' she whispered, wishing desperately she could take her eyes away.

'It wasn't taken,' said Jason. 'Whatever was in there . . . it escaped.'

Diesel sat bolt upright in her bed, her heart thumping violently, wide awake. What a horrible dream! But was it a dream, or a memory? When she looked back at the scene by that opened grave this afternoon, was it *true* that she had found herself staring very hard at the coffin lid? Was it *true* that she had seen just exactly what the dream had shown her? The nails sticking straight up? Had she noticed then (though she had shoved the thought away from her, refused to look at it), that the coffin lid *seemed to have been opened from the inside?* The thing inside, the thing that was only an empty dead body, had not been stolen. It had escaped. Had that thought been in her mind before she slept?

Oh no, no, it couldn't be. It was simply a nightmare. She lay down and closed her eyes, glad that such a terrible idea could not be true.

Strangely, she fell asleep again quite quickly. The shock of the discovery at the ruins, and the effort of trying to behave normally for Mum and Dad when she came home, had left her exhausted. She was too worn out to be frightened by a dream. She fell asleep again: and dreamed this time about Martin.

This dream took her back to their first days in number 57. She was out in the garden with her mum and dad. Michael, their neighbour from number 59, the man who lived alone with his fussy mother, was warning them against the Knight brothers. 'That's the way they'll do it,' he said, pointing up at the back wall of the house. 'Over their wall and up your drainpipe easy-peasy: break a bedroom window if they can't get it open, and make off with anything they can get their hands on.'

It had never happened. The Knight boys had never broken into number 55. But in Diesel's dream, she was suddenly not in the garden but in bed: and that was the way Martin came into her room. Over the wall and up the drainpipe. He didn't have to break the window, because Diesel slept with her window open in the summer. He slipped inside, and came and sat on the end of her bed. She knew it was Martin, though of course she couldn't see him. The room was dark, and she had her eyes shut.

'Don't open your eyes,' he said; and it was Martin's voice.

'I won't,' said Diesel.

'Whatever you do, don't open your eyes. Promise.'

'I promise.' Martin was dead, but he sounded so real. 'Can I touch you?'

'No. Better not.'

'But you can talk to me?'

'Yes. I've come to talk to you. I don't want to scare you Diesel, but I really need to talk to someone about what's happening to me.'

'That's okay.'

'Well.' Martin sighed. He sounded tired and sad, as if coming back from the dead was a long, dreary journey. 'You saw me, didn't you? You saw me in the church that night. Do you mind talking about this?'

'I don't mind. Whatever you want.'

'I know you didn't want to believe it was me, but it was. Somehow I'm not dead. Or I'm dead but . . . walking. I was wondering if you could help me understand why I'm like this.'

'Yes,' whispered Diesel. 'I'll try.'

'It's to do with that grave. Your brain doesn't work very well when you're dead . . . but I know what's happened to me is something to do with that particular grave. The one in the ruined church, where you and John and Jason buried me. I'm not blaming you. It was a nice gesture. But it didn't work out too well. Don't open your eyes, Diesel. Please don't.'

'I won't. Could you hold my hand?'

She heard him move, quickly, shifting out of her reach. Even if she stretched out her arms now, she wouldn't be able to touch him. She could imagine him shaking his head, and smiling that hopeless smile: his face white and tired, the dark limp fringe flopping in his eyes.

'Better not,' he whispered.

'It was the ghoul's grave,' said Diesel. 'It was where Abbot Roger reburied his zombie.'

'Who's Abbot Roger?'

'A medieval magician,' said Diesel. 'He made the dead body of a criminal into a guardian for the Abbey treasure. But the monster he made got out of control and turned into a ghoul, preying on the living and the dead. So he undid his spells, or he tried to; and reburied the body in the church, on holy ground. And then we came along. We buried you in the ghoul's grave. It was a terrible mistake: but we didn't know.'

In her dream she knew. She could see in her mind, clear as day, the carving of the Sanctuary Knocker, the sign the Abbot magician had ordered to be carved on the monster's gravestone; to mark a place where evil was supposed to be safely contained, like a criminal in sanctuary.

'*Non licet perturbari.* That's what it said. It's Latin. It means, this stone must not be disturbed.'

'Oh,' said Martin. 'I see. Pity my brother couldn't read Latin, when he was looking for a nice peaceful resting place . . . But Diesel, there wasn't any ghoul in there with me. I would have noticed.'

'There was nothing in the grave,' said Diesel. 'No bones, nothing. Jason told me that. Of course there wasn't. The zombie had rotted away, until there was nothing left of him but dust, dust mixed in with the soil. Abbot Roger had tried to undo the spell, but he didn't succeed. I don't know if the zombie really went on walking. Maybe that was only a story the bad friars told, to scare people. But the spell was still there, making the place bad. And it was strongest in the dust that had once been the zombie's body. I know it was, because it worked on you.'

She was troubled by the smell that had come into her room with him. She wasn't going to mention it. She was going to ignore it, and refuse to notice it at all. The fact that Martin was here talking to her was much more important.

'Okay,' said Martin. 'That explains a few things. But the nasty thing is . . . Well, at first I was trying to get back somewhere. I didn't know where I was trying to get to, but I knew I had this mission. I used to sneak in and out of that grave really carefully – I didn't want anyone to know what had happened to me – and go searching around in the dark. Like Count Dracula, getting in and out of his coffin. But that's changed. I don't want to scare you, Diesel. But if you know all this stuff about ghouls and zombies, then I'll tell you. I'm getting so I don't want to go back to my grave at all. I keep having ideas about . . . hunting and eating and I don't want to say *what* I want to eat. I'm afraid I'm changing into a . . . a what you said. A monster.'

Diesel sat up. She held out her arms. She had been trying to keep very calm, but these words were too much for her. 'Oh, *Martin*—'

'Don't open your eyes!' he cried, and again she knew he'd moved, almost flung himself away from her, as if in horror at the thought of her touch.

But she had kept her promise. Her eyes were still closed. She lay back.

'Diesel, are you crying?'

'I'm sorry, I am a bit.'

'Please don't cry, because . . . please don't cry.'

'We'll take the spell off you. We'll get an exorcist.'

'I don't think so, Diesel. I don't know about your Abbot Roger, but what's happening to me feels really powerful. I don't believe any old minister lighting a few candles and thinking holy thoughts is going to touch this. You'd have to be a saint or something . . . Or else a major-league top magician that knows all about how to defuse powerful medieval spells, and where are you going to find one of those? Nowhere. I'm done for.'

'No, Martin. I won't believe that.'

'Don't open your eyes.'

'I wasn't going to.'

'It's no use, Diesel. I was done for before I died. You tried, but there was no use anyone trying to help me then, and there is no use you trying to help me now. I just wanted to talk to you really, before . . . you know. While I'm still me. Now I'd better go.'

She sat up again. Her eyes were closed, but she couldn't stop herself from reaching out to him, once more: 'Martin, please don't go. Stay, talk to me. We'll think of a way out.'

'No we won't, because there isn't one. I'd better go, because you're going to wake up if I stay, and I *really* don't want that to happen. Good night, Diesel. Take care.'

She felt that the weight of the person sitting on the end of her bed was gone. Martin stood up, slipped out of the window, and was gone.

Then Diesel slept, and did not remember anything more.

She woke up when her alarm went off, and lay there in the cruel moment when you wake remembering something terrible and unchangeable has happened, but you don't know what it is. Oh yes, Martin is dead . . . But she was used to this cruel moment of waking. It came less often now, as the thought of Martin dead became fixed and accepted in her mind. Then she remembered the dream.

She sat up, tears stinging her eyes. She had never dreamed of him like that before. She'd hardly dreamed of him at all, except a few little fragments: Martin's face and smile glimpsed in the stupid usual kind of dream about flying crocodiles on a school trip, or whatever. It was a miserable shame that when she *did* dream of him, it had to be all mixed up with the horrible ghoul story. But that's what dreams are like. They're patched together out of the strangest bits and pieces. At least she had heard his voice again. She reached under her pillow for a tissue to wipe her eyes. That was when she noticed the faint, horrible smell that seemed to be clinging to her bedcovers.

Her window was open. The foul smell of something dead and rotten was in her room. The fresh air from the open window had blown it away, but not entirely . . .

Diesel leapt out of bed, and rushed to the bathroom. Just got there in time. She was violently sick. She crouched on the bathroom floor in a cold sweat, shaking all over.

'Diesel?' Her mother was knocking on the door. 'Diesel, are you all right?'

'No. I've been sick.'

The door wasn't locked. Her mother came in, knelt

down and put her arm around Diesel's shoulders, helped her up and got her a glass of water; felt her forehead.

'What happened, baby? Have you been ill in the night?'

'No,' she whispered. 'I woke up, and I suddenly had to be sick.'

'Well, you haven't got a fever. Does your head ache? Does your stomach hurt?'

'Nothing like that,' muttered Diesel – although her head was aching fit to burst. 'I'm all right. I was sick, it's over.'

'Maybe something she ate,' said her dad, coming to the bathroom door fastening his tie.

'You don't *look* as if it's over,' said Mum. 'You're very shaky. You go back to bed.'

'No! I'll be all right. I'm going to school.'

Her parents thought she was behaving extremely strangely. They didn't understand that she was frantic to get *away* from that bedroom, from this house; from all reminders of what had come to her in the night. She refused to let her mother take her temperature or put her back to bed. She forced herself to dress and get ready for school. She even tried to force herself to eat, while her mum and dad watched with worried, wondering eyes. But that was impossible. She could not eat, she would choke. She would throw up again.

'Diesel, is there something deadly important going on at school today?'

'Have you got a lesson with that Geography teacher you girls all think is so cute?' suggested her dad, with a grin. 'The poor man—'

'No! I just don't like being ill. I hate staying in bed. I'll be okay, honestly.'

'She's never liked being ill,' said her dad. He always

111

defended Diesel, when her mum wanted to play the heavy parent. 'I expect it's nothing. If she starts feeling bad again in school, she can get a taxi home.'

While Diesel tried to sip some tea, she heard them muttering to each other in the hall as Dad was going off to work. They were almost laughing, about the mysterious and ridiculous behaviour of teenage girls. She went to school, and survived the day, took the bus and walked home from her bus stop in the usual way.

The sickness and shock had passed. She knew there had not really been a dead body in her room last night, sitting on the end of her bed and talking to her. If she had woken, *if she had opened her eyes*, the room would have been empty. Surely it would have been empty! But sometimes a dream will make sense of something you knew, that you didn't understand while you were awake. *Non licet perturbari* . . . and the carving of the sanctuary knocker. Yes, she thought. What I told Martin in the dream is true. We buried him in the ghoul's grave. It was obvious, now she came to think of it.

But *what about the rest?* The terrible, unbearable, nightmare part?

She had walked through Chapterhouse Mall, without realising what she was doing. It was the route she had been avoiding since Martin died. Out in the plaza the sun was shining, it was warm, there were lots of people in summer clothes: bare arms, bare legs, bare shoulders. She came to the Elephant Fountain, and Martin was sitting there, in his frayed jeans and an old green Umbro shirt, waiting to watch her go by . . .

Not the Martin of the dream. The Martin of memory . . .

But while the Martin of her memories smiled at her, she

was looking at the people around her, and thinking of the Martin in her dream. The Martin who was afraid he was turning into a monster. All that plump flesh, brown flesh, pink flesh, pale flesh . . . She had to run into the public toilets, and throw up.

Don't open your eyes, he had said.

But I have to open my eyes, she thought. I have to know.

She went home, struggled through her tea, and went out again. She took the last bus of the evening out to Browclough. It dropped her in the village at about 9 p.m. She walked to the ruins alone. It was still light. This was bad, because she had to wait for darkness. She couldn't stand to wait in the ruined church, or the cloisters. She went to the lime avenue, and sat there under a tree. In the deepening twilight the old limes were great towers of foliage, like tall green clouds. The secret canal was here, underground: running through that cave with its strange shaft of light, where Martin had liked to hide. When she listened hard she thought she could hear the sound of strong-flowing water, mingling with the endless murmur of the leaves. An owl hooted, a bat flickered across her view of the ruins like an abrupt black butterfly. Stars came out. Everything was so quiet that she could hear the sheep, still awake, cropping the turf around the old stones.

Somewhere between deepest twilight and real dark, she dozed off.

She woke up cold, stiffly curled up between the roots of the lime tree. She felt like a chilled, dried-out dead animal. She'd brought a torch with her. She switched it on, and went to see if she could find the ghoul.

In the ruined church, the stone marked NON LICET PERTURBARI was back in its place. The light of her torch trembled as it played over the carving of the Sanctuary Knocker; her hand was shaking. She wondered what this meant. In the dream, Martin had said that he no longer felt he had to go back to his grave during the day. She remembered the stone thrown aside, the coffin defiantly ripped open; signs that the ghoul had broken free from that prison. It didn't have to stay in sanctuary any more. But then who had replaced the stone? She was plunged deeper into fear. Maybe the gravestone had never been moved. What was dream and what was real? She pinched herself, and it hurt, but that could be part of the dream too. Maybe she was lying in her own bed right this minute, having one of those nightmares where you try and try but you can't wake up.

But she must wake up. She must get free of this nightmare, and save Martin.

Think! Think! It has broken loose, the protection isn't working. Maybe it was clever enough to come back and hide the traces of its escape. So where is it now? It gets restless, *it goes hunting*. She ran out of the church, her fists pressed to her mouth to stop herself from screaming, because now there was no use saying *it was only a dream*. There was no difference between reality and dreaming, in this nightmare that had swallowed her, and she knew Martin had really come to her last night . . . Martin's trapped and tainted spirit had really come to her in that dream. And what he'd told her was true. It was happening. Martin's spirit was trapped in his own dead body, turning into a monster.

She ran and ran, stumbling over low walls, falling into turfy ditches. Blurred shapes loomed, the door to the great kitchen opened in front of her like a great black mouth. At last, by the big barnlike shape of the dormitorium, she managed to stop herself. She stood leaning against the ancient stonework with her eyes closed, seeing in her mind the figure she had seen by moonlight, that night when she'd come out here with Jason. The dead face she had glimpsed . . . and afterwards refused to admit what she had seen.

Oh, but it would be worse now. The body had been dead for longer.

But she was wasting time. It didn't have to stay here, it could go anywhere it liked as long as it stayed within the abbey's old boundaries. The creature that used to be Martin had gone to find the flesh that would satisfy its hunger. She began to run again, out past the ticket booth, along the footpath. She reached the gate into the lane, her throat burning. Flung herself over the stile on to the grassy verge.

How could she find the monster? It could be anywhere.

Then she realised she could smell that charnel smell, the smell of something long dead. It was like a fresh trail in the air. She looked up and saw something walking along the lane ahead, a shambling dim figure that she could barely make out in the darkness. It was walking away from her, towards Browclough. She must follow, but she was so frightened she couldn't move. What was she going to do if she caught up with it? What could she possibly do? She heard the sound of a car. It came around the bend: a pair of headlights leapt into view, blinding her. She heard the car slow down. She couldn't see a thing, but she knew what the driver must have seen . . . a swaying, shambling human figure, walking right down the middle of the road. The car was stopping. The driver had not noticed Diesel, but it had seen someone apparently in trouble, and was stopping to find out what was wrong. In the old days, lonely travellers on this road by night would have known they'd better not stop for *any* reason . . .

She began to run, shouting 'Don't stop! Don't stop! *Go on*, get away from here!'

She was running towards the thing. She was going to catch up with it, the dead thing walking, the creature in the picture she had copied. She was going to see its face, the face of the dead thing. The headlight dazzle was still in her eyes, but in a moment she was going to see it. The darkness was not dark enough to save her from what she knew she must do, she must *look* this time. She must force herself to see the horror clearly, to know the worst.

The car's engine growled, it gathered speed again and zoomed away. The creature had turned, as if it had heard Diesel shouting. She stopped. She could not make herself go on. It was almost invisible, dark against the darkness; but she seemed to see it leap, moving with great speed and strength, over the hedge by the side of the road and into the field beyond.

It was gone. Diesel was left standing, shaking, realising for the first time that she had dropped her torch in the ruins. It was the middle of the night. She didn't have much money with her, she didn't know how she was going to get home. She started walking, and walked straight into someone, who must have come up while she was staring after the monster. Hands gripped her arms. She yelled, and struggled; but he was bigger than her and much stronger.

'Diesel! Diesel! Shut up, stop that, it's me—'

It was Jason Knight.

'What are you doing here?' she cried.

'What are *you* doing here? In the middle of the night?'

'I was looking for Martin.'

She dropped down, and sat on the edge of the verge, in the long summer grass, her head between her knees. After a moment the faintness passed. She looked up. Jason was sitting beside her, a shadow against the night.

'I came back,' he said. 'I kept thinking about that open grave, I knew we couldn't leave that gaping hole. Hardly anyone comes here, but the farmer who lets the sheep in might have noticed it. I couldn't leave John last night, he was too upset. I've had to leave him tonight, I hope he hasn't woken. I managed to shove the slab back in place.'

'So it was you who did that,' whispered Diesel. 'I thought it must have been the ghoul.'

'Stop talking like that.'

'*You know it's true.* You saw the handprint. You saw that the coffin hadn't been opened from the outside. It was pushed open, by something inside.'

'Just *stop it* Diesel. You're going to drive yourself crazy.'

'It is true,' she insisted, so full of fear and horror she didn't care what she was saying. 'You said we'd seen Martin's ghost that night, and I knew you were right but I refused to admit it. But the real truth is much worse. We buried him in the grave where the ghoul was buried, and the old spell was still in there, in the earth. You know how he was killed. *He was a criminal and he died by violence!* He meets the conditions of the spell. He has become the ghoul.'

'I was the one that buried him there,' said Martin's brother, as if the words were forced out of him. 'You said we should put him somewhere else. I remember that. But I wouldn't listen.'

'I didn't think things like this could happen. I thought God wouldn't allow it. But if someone dies in a state of despair, then evil can get hold of them. That's what's happened to Martin, and I don't know why you won't admit it. I know you never wanted me to be friends with him. Now you're trying to pretend this unbelievably terrible situation doesn't exist. *When you know it is real!* You're supposed to care about your brothers. That's what people say. No matter what else he's done, Jason Knight cares about his brothers. But you *don't*. If you cared, you'd be trying to help me think of a way to save him. Instead of dismissing everything I do, as if I'm worthless!'

Jason didn't say anything, but she could hear him breathing hard, like someone in a rage. She was afraid he was going to hit her, or yell at her. He didn't. He stood up. 'It's true, I didn't want you being friends with Martin. I'm sorry. I was afraid it would lead to trouble . . . for you. It's the middle of the night. You shouldn't be out here. I shouldn't have got you involved. I must have been mad. You thought you saw something that night when I brought you here, but it was the power of suggestion. Best if you forget all about it.'

'I saw something again, tonight.'

'I told you. Power of suggestion. Listen, moving the coffin was a daft idea. Now somebody with a grudge against the Knight brothers has taken Martin's body. That's all. I don't know what I'm going to do about it, but it's not your problem. I want you to *forget the whole thing*. Do yourself a favour, forget you ever met us. Come on, the car's down the road. I'll take you home.'

It was well past midnight when they reached Linden Grove. The lights were shining through the front curtains of Diesel's house. The door opened as she got out of the car. Dad stood there, and looked very hard and grimly at Jason, but he didn't say anything. Jason didn't say good night. Diesel went into the house, and Dad shut the door behind her. Everything looked unnaturally bright indoors, after so much darkness.

'What time do you call this?' Dad shouted.

'I'm sorry Dad.'

'Do you realise we might have called the police! What do you think you've been doing? I can't believe it! It's outrageous!'

'We called Bev's mum,' said Mum, coming out into the hall. 'And Anita's house. We'll have to call them again, tell them you came home all right.'

'You know what Bev's mum said to me,' yelled Dad. 'She said, why worry? An inconsiderate teenager stays out after bedtime without calling home: that's normal behaviour. I said *you don't know my Diesel*.' He glared at her, 'Maybe *I* don't know my Diesel, anymore.'

'I said I'm sorry, Dad.'

'You could have called us, Diesel,' said Mum. 'We had no idea where you were.'

'I didn't think—'

'Oh, I see,' yelled Dad. 'You *didn't think*! Fine! Great! What were you doing out with that Knight boy anyway. What kind of company is that for a girl your age, a boy like that?'

'I wasn't—'

She'd started to say *I wasn't with him*, but realised that would only make things worse.

'I have no patience with this kind of behaviour. Self-centred, heartless—'

'Oh baby,' said her mum, putting her arms round Diesel. There were tears in Mum's eyes. 'What is *happening* to you?'

Four

Diesel's dad had never spoken to her like that before. It hurt her, in the middle of all her other trouble, that Dad would be so quick to shout and yell and believe she'd been doing wrong. But by morning he'd calmed down. They both talked to her, over breakfast, about trust and consideration. Dad said he *did* trust her, but she had to accept that coming back after midnight, when she hadn't even said where she was going, was completely out of order.

'I couldn't help it, Dad. I'm very sorry. We were out for a drive, and talking, and we . . . we had car trouble. It won't happen again, honest.'

She hated lying, but she had to lie. There was no way she could tell them the truth!

'Well, you could have found a phone, I'm sure. I'm surprised at Jason, too. Don't you ever be so hard on your poor old parents again. You must admit I had a right to be upset.'

Diesel listened, and nodded, and agreed. She wondered what they'd think if she explained. If she told them she had gone out to the Abbey ruins and stayed there for hours alone, chasing a nightmare, so full of fear and dread that an idea like *my parents will worry* had never entered her mind.

After Dad had gone out to work her mum said, 'Diesel, I know these days fourteen isn't too young to have a boyfriend. And I know that you weren't doing anything you shouldn't, no matter how late you stayed out: because I know you. But Jason is nearly eighteen. That's a big gap, at your age. I'm not saying anything against him. I believe there's a very decent, very mature young man under all the wildness. But he's too old for you.'

Diesel stared at her. 'It's not like that,' she said at last. She couldn't say *I don't even like him*, not now. So she had to tell another lie. 'We're friends.'

Life got worse for Diesel after that, in every way . . . Just one late night and her parents started treating her like a criminal. It wasn't the way they had yelled at her when she came home after midnight. It was the way they *watched* her. Whenever she looked up, there would be Mum and Dad staring – as if they thought she'd do something terrible if they took their eyes off her for a moment. If she stayed in her room it was worse, they'd keep making excuses to come and look in, and then she'd quickly have to pretend to be doing something, although really all she would have been doing was staring at the wall. It was the same at school. Her friends were giving her worried looks, and she was sure they were talking about her behind her back. Teachers who had always treated her with respect started nagging her, and getting sharp with her when she answered back; first sharp then *watchful*, like her mum and dad.

Of course she knew why everyone was treating her like this. She knew she'd become silent and withdrawn and sulky, totally unlike herself. But she couldn't help feeling angry with them, because *they wouldn't leave her alone.*

She couldn't concentrate in her classes, she didn't get much homework done. She kept waking up in the morning and thinking she could smell that horrible smell – in her bedroom, in the bathroom, while she was trying to eat breakfast. She knew it was in her mind, because Mum and Dad never said anything about it. But when she woke up haunted by the smell of death, she was sure it meant she had dreamed of Martin again. That made her so frightened. If he could only come to her in dreams, and she forgot the dreams when she woke up, he could be telling her something vital, something that would help her to rescue him, and she would never know.

She watched the local news programmes with terrible attention, and started buying the local papers every day. They piled up in her room, she read them when she was supposed to be doing homework. About a week after that night out at the ruins, the thing she had been most dreading happened. She found a report, in the *Moorland Gazette*, about something shocking that had happened in a village churchyard. The village wasn't Browclough. It was somewhere called Drent, about five miles from the Abbey ruins; but she was sure it was well within the old boundaries of the Abbey's land.

An old lady had died, and been buried. Three days after they buried her, a local naturalist had been on his way home in the middle of the night. He'd been watching for badgers, and having no luck. He'd seen something moving in the village churchyard. Not thinking anything was wrong he'd gone in, hoping he was going to see a wild animal, a fox or a deer or a badger. What he'd seen was a coffin pulled out of the ground, and 'a human figure' bending over it. Mr Benson, the naturalist, had yelled, the figure had run away. Mr Benson had given chase, but the intruder had escaped. The police said Mr Benson had been brave but foolish. This new and nasty kind of vandalism was probably the work of troubled teenagers, maybe on drugs, and they could be dangerous.

She'd bought the paper on her way to school. She forced herself to go on, go into school as usual: but when she got there she felt so sick she had to go and throw up before her first lesson. Then she had to leave that lesson, because she couldn't stop crying.

Mum and Dad and the teachers made her have an appointment with the school counsellor, hoping it would be easier for her to talk to someone other than her parents. They didn't understand that Diesel wasn't refusing to talk to them out of defiance or because she didn't trust them. It was because she couldn't, *couldn't, couldn't* tell anyone what was wrong. She knew now that her plan of telling Mum and Dad the whole story, and asking them to help her find an exorcist, was hopeless and crazy. No one could help her. The interview didn't go well. Diesel was so tired of being watched and worried about that she gave the counsellor sour back-answers or no answers at all. Was she taking illegal drugs? asked the nice gentle lady. She put it kindly, but that was what she meant.

'No,' said Diesel. 'I wish I was, but I don't think it would help.'

'Do you have any reason to be worrying that you might be pregnant?'

'I don't think so. I'm a virgin, and I haven't been talking to any angels.'

She knew she was talking herself down, but she couldn't stop.

It was funny, in a sick sort of way. It was like everybody had said at the start, those Knight brothers were nothing but trouble. If Diesel had never had anything to do with them, she would have been fine. Now it was too late to turn back. Too late to undo what had been done, too late to escape from the horror.

By this stage she had no chance to dream of Martin, because she didn't sleep. She didn't eat much, either. She was afraid she was going to have a nervous breakdown, if she didn't think of an answer soon.

There must be an answer. There *must*.

Finally it came to her. The glimmering of a horrible idea.

She hadn't seen or spoken to the brothers since the night Jason had brought her home from the ruins. John wasn't friends with her anymore. When he saw her in the street in town he'd cross over the road. If he was out in front of the house when she came by he'd dart indoors when he saw her coming. Jason was avoiding her too. He must have found somewhere else to work on his cars, he was never outside the front of number 55. She'd been glad they weren't talking to her, glad she didn't have to talk to them; though she was sorry about John. But when she'd thought of her horrible idea, she had to tell someone.

Her mum had kept her off school that day, and taken the day off work herself. Mum said it was because the DIY work at home was getting on top of her, and she needed to sort it out. Diesel knew her mum was hoping to get her to open up and confess what was wrong . . . but it wasn't going to work, especially not now she'd had her idea. She absolutely *couldn't* tell Mum what was going through her mind! At least they got plenty of decorating work done. They spent the morning varnishing the new cork floor in the kitchen. After lunch they started stripping the walls in the bathroom, which was the next room due for its dream-house makeover. Diesel thought the hard work might make her feel better, but it didn't. She would find herself standing, staring at the scraper in her hand; and realise her mum had stopped work too, and was *watching* . . . Leave me alone!, she wanted to shout.

But she didn't yell or break down. She managed to behave fairly normally. She ate some lunch, although it nearly choked her. Late in the afternoon she managed to sneak out. The orange MGB wasn't outside number 55. She hoped that meant Jason wasn't around.

She knocked hard on the door without a doorbell. John answered. He was looking rough. His school uniform looked as if it had been slept in, he was wearing a grubby T-shirt instead of a shirt and he was very pale. The hallway of the house smelled of stale food and spilled beer again, and there was the old confusion of litter and dirty clothes lying around.

He stared unhappily when he saw who it was, but he said, 'Come in.'

'You've given up trying to keep the place clean,' said Diesel.

'It's Jason,' said John. 'I do my best, but he says what's the point. He's been dead rude to Mrs Goodyear too.'

'Maybe you'll be taken into care after all,' said Diesel. John looked shocked, but she couldn't help it. She hadn't any spare energy for not hurting people's feelings. 'Is Jason here?' she asked, glancing suspiciously around.

'No. I dunno where he is.'

They went into the front room, which was also in a mess. There was a pile of local newspapers on the floor. Diesel stared at them. 'Have you been reading those?'

'No,' said John, puzzled. 'Jason suddenly started buying them.'

I know why, thought Diesel.

'He's told you not to be friends with me anymore, hasn't he.'

John nodded. 'I'm sorry Diesel. He says it's for the best. He says we can only rely on each other. That's the way it's always been, and always will be. You're too different from us.'

She looked around the miserable scruffy room. 'It doesn't look to me as if you can rely on Jason to look after you, not by the state of things in here. Doesn't he want you to have any other friends but him?'

'It's not like that. You don't understand. His enemies took Martin's body, and he's concentrating on finding out who did it. When he's sorted that out, we'll be fine.'

'Has he done anything about "sorting" it? Or getting Martin back?'

John shook his head, looking at the floor. 'I don't think so. Not yet.'

'That's because it wasn't Jason's enemies who took Martin, John. Your brother knows it. He doesn't want to face up to the truth. But we have to.'

She looked again at the pile of local papers. She couldn't tell John the worst part, but she would tell him something. 'Do you . . . do you dream about him? Martin?'

He shrugged. 'Maybe. I've had a lot of nightmares since he got killed. But I never remember them when I wake up.'

Diesel swallowed hard. 'I've got an idea. That's what I came to talk to you about. It's a mad idea, but it might work. First, you've got to tell me you believe me when I say *Jason is lying*. There were no bodysnatchers. There's a ghoul. It haunts the ruins: that's really true.'

John stared at her miserably. 'I know,' he said, in a husky whisper. 'I can tell by the way Jason is. He wouldn't be this upset if it was only some dirty rotten practical joke. And he'd have *done* something. But he's not *lying*. He doesn't want me to be scared.'

'I don't want you to be scared either. But we have to talk about this. I think there is a way to . . . to save Martin from the ghoul. We can make the rules of the spell work for us. The spell works on *the body of a criminal died by violence*. Supposing we could get *one of those*? And we put it in the haunted grave?'

'What, so the ghoul would take *that* body an' all? What good would that do?'

She could not tell him that his brother had become the ghoul. 'Well, it would be a *better* dead body. More of a criminal than Martin was. If it had a better dead body, the ghoul might put Martin's body back.'

John screwed up his face, trying to make sense of this idea. 'Where were you going to get this dead body of a criminal?'

'I don't know . . . I thought, could we burgle the police morgue?'

'I think you're going crazy, Diesel.'

'Yes,' she said, wiping away some tears. 'I think I am.' She had known her idea wouldn't make sense to John. But Jason would understand.

'Just tell your brother,' she said. 'Tell Jason what I said, that's all.'

'Tell Jason what?'

Jason Knight was standing in the door to the room, leaning against the wall with his arms folded. Neither of them had heard him come in. 'You left the front door open,' he said. He gave Diesel a hard, unfriendly look. 'I told you to stay away from us.'

'Diesel says we should get a criminal's body, and bury it in the ruins,' said John. 'And then whatever took Martin would let him go. She thinks you could burgle the police morgue, like you did the cemetery. I don't get it, but that's what she thinks.'

Jason stared at Diesel. She couldn't tell what was going through his head. He was as pale and scruffy as John, and there were red rims to his eyes again; but his only expression was the same old scorn for Diesel and her suggestions. 'Thanks,' he said coldly. 'That's a great idea. Funny thing is, it's a lot like an idea I've had myself. Now you can go. Go on, go. Get back to your nice life. I told you, I don't want you involved in our business. Whatever happened, I mean *whatever* happened, to our Martin, I'll sort it myself.'

'Okay,' said Diesel. 'But if I can help you, I'll do anything. I don't care how horrible.' She walked past him, feeling despairing. Jason was right to be scornful, robbing the police morgue was a stupid, insane idea. But having ordered her out, he then followed her into the hall. She jumped and flinched when he took hold of her arm.

'It's okay,' he said quietly. 'I'm not going to hit you. I wanted to say, I've got a better plan. I know how to set him free. If I need your help, I'll let you know. Okay? Now get out of here, before your dad comes after me with a shotgun.'

129

She went back to number 57.

'Where've you been, Diesel?' asked her mum.

'I went out for a breath of air,' snapped Diesel. 'Why can't you leave me alone!'

She stormed up to her room, and lay on the bed. It was a comfort to think that there was somebody else who *knew* what she was going through, although it was Jason Knight. Everyone else except John, all the people around her, would be sure she was out of her mind if she started talking about corpse-stealing ghouls. No one else in the world, not even John, would ever know, could ever be told, the final, terrible secret of what had happened to Martin . . . She wondered what Jason was going to do. She had a bad feeling about his plan, especially the fact that he'd said it was like her own horrible idea. Was he really going to try and get hold of 'a better dead body'? How could he possibly manage that?

Don't open your eyes.

Diesel's eyes flew open. She was lying in her bed. The room was empty, except for the faint, foul smell of something long dead, which only existed in Diesel's mind. The dream had vanished, and she remembered nothing.

I have to find a way, she thought. I have to find a way for you to reach me . . .

Today was Saturday. The day she'd taken off school had been Monday. She had been better, since then. Nothing was solved, but she seemed to have found a reserve of strength. Mum and Dad had started looking relieved; although they still crept around her as if they were walking on eggshells. But today there was no school, and she didn't know how to fill the blank hours. She didn't want to go out, she didn't want to meet her friends.

In the end she spent the day helping her dad with the new tiling around the bath, while her mum painted the bathroom woodwork in a lovely bright blue gloss. They kept themselves going with chocolate bars and sausage sandwiches, listened to Radio One and sang along with the silliest summer pop songs. The three of them were almost a happy family again; sometimes Diesel actually laughed. But all the while she was thinking of ways and means to let Martin's spirit come to her, to let him speak to her so that she could remember, instead of losing everything when she woke up from her haunted dreams.

At last Mum and Dad called a halt to the decorating and went out to the supermarket for the week's shopping. Diesel came along, which was something she hadn't done in a long time, and then they all three cooked a meal together. It was quite easy to behave normally, because *she had thought of a way*. A safe way . . . Now she only had to get out of the house, without them being worried. In the end she decided the simplest approach was best. She went up to her room and came down again dressed to go out.

'I thought I might go and see Anita. I won't be late, is that all right?'

Diesel's friend Anita lived a few streets away. She hoped her parents would be so relieved by the way she'd been behaving today that they'd be ashamed to ask suspicious questions; or make her call Anita first. Sure enough, they fell for it. They looked at each other, and Mum nodded.

'Be back by ten,' said her dad. 'Okay?'

'I hear you.'

I didn't lie, she thought, as she left the house. I only said I *thought* I might go to see Anita, I only said '*I hear you,*' when he said back by ten.

But of course she would be back, no problem there . . .

She went to the Chapterhouse Mall. It was a fine summer evening, sunny and warm. Some shops were still open, but the shopping crowds had begun to thin out. The violinist busking outside British Home Stores was playing something classical; that was beautiful but very sad. Diesel went to sit on the edge of the Elephant Fountain, choosing the exact spot where Martin had so often waited, doing nothing much, until Diesel walked by. She was glad it was evening. There were fewer people, and not so much risk of meeting any of her schoolfriends. The fountain murmured behind her. The westering sun fell full on her face, warm as if she was looking into a fire.

She thought she ought to be praying to God, but all she could manage was something like praying to Martin. Come to me now, she begged him silently. I know you've been coming to me in my dreams, I know you must be trying to tell me something, but *I can't remember the dreams.* I wake up and they are gone. I'll close my eyes. I promise I won't open my eyes. She thought of the smile she used to call Martin's hopeless smile. But Martin had not been completely hopeless. He would say things like 'no one can help me, I'm a disaster'; and then he would do things like taking Diesel out to the Abbey ruins, like kissing her, like standing with her by the riverside, stroking the cherry blossom petals from her hair. No matter what he *said*, Martin had never quite given up hope while he was alive. He died in a bad state of mind, she thought, but *he didn't die in despair.* There was still a spark. He can be saved.

You know something, she told him, in her mind. There's

something that you're trying to tell me. This is one of our places. If you can visit my dreams, you must be able to reach me here too. Please, come to me now, while I'm awake, so I'll be able to remember . . . Nothing happened, except that the warmth of the sun slowly moved across her cheeks and was gone. At last she opened her eyes, feeling bitterly disappointed.

Across the square she saw Jason Knight, walking with his shoulders hunched and his head down. He was carrying a black sports bag, but it looked as if the bag was empty. She jumped up. He hadn't seen her. He looked as if he was trying not to be noticed, as if he was doing something secret. On an impulse, she followed him.

The atmosphere of the town centre had changed. A different crowd was coming out. People were gathering outside the pubs, sitting at outdoor tables drinking and laughing. Diesel followed Jason across the bridge and uphill, into the older shopping streets around the cathedral. It wasn't hard to keep him in sight without being spotted, because he looked neither to right or left; he marched straight on, mechanically, like a wind-up toy. Finally he went into a pub on the corner of a narrow alley. It was called the Counting House. It didn't *look* different from any other pub, but the men hanging around the door and sitting on the steps outside – there were no tables, and there were no women – stared at Diesel suspiciously. You could see they thought she was somewhere she didn't belong. She crossed the street, and pretended to check out the clothes in the window of a little funky-fashion shop. If he stayed in there for hours, she would have to give up and go home.

But he didn't. About ten minutes later he came out again and set off back the way he'd come, walking with the same mechanical speed. He was still carrying the black sports bag, and it still seemed to be empty. She'd started to wonder why she was trailing him, but then she glimpsed his face, reflected in a shop window as they both passed by, a few paces apart. He was very pale and his expression was grim. Suddenly she was certain he was on his way to do something terrible, and she had to stop him.

She hurried to catch up. 'Jason!'

He stopped and turned round. 'Diesel,' he said, looking disgusted.

'Where are you going? What were you doing in that pub?'

'What pub?' He scowled. 'Have you been following me?'

'You told me you had a plan. *What are you planning to do*?'

'Go home, Diesel. Stop following me around, you stupid kid.'

'If it's to do with Martin, I have a right to know. Maybe I can help.'

He laughed. 'No one can help me with this. Go home, forget you saw me.'

'No, I won't! I know you need me! You promised you'd come to me for help.'

They were standing in the middle of the pavement. People passing by gave them curious glances. 'You're going to ruin everything,' said Jason, but he looked less angry. 'I can't stand here talking. Okay, you want to help. You can help—'

'Then tell me! Tell me what I can do!'

'Look out for John-boy. If I can't take care of him any more, don't you give up on him. Visit him, keep in touch, promise me you'll do that.'

'Of course I would. But no one's going to split you and John up.'

Jason shrugged. 'It might happen.'

'I know you're going to do something crazy. I don't want to get you in trouble, but if you won't tell me about it, I'm going to talk to your social worker. I saw you go into the Counting House. That's a place where really dodgy characters hang out, isn't it? I'm going to call Mrs Goodyear, and tell her you've been hanging around a criminals' pub.'

He looked *very* angry then, so she knew she'd guessed the truth. 'Tell her what you like. It's not going to make any difference.'

'I'll tell her anyway. I'll find a phonebox and call her *now*.'

She didn't know how she was going to contact the social worker, she just said that to try and get through to him. It was a mistake. As she spoke she saw something change in his eyes, like *snap*. She only had a moment's warning: it wasn't enough. He grabbed her by the wrist, while his other hand whipped round her back and took hold of her free arm in a fierce hard grip. She could struggle, but she couldn't get away without a fight.

'Okay,' he said, savagely. 'You can come with me. Or you can start yelling and screaming, and stop me from doing the one thing that will help Martin. Your choice.'

Diesel didn't make a sound. He marched her, keeping that tight grip on her all the way, into a side street, where a white BMW was parked by the kerb. He opened the passenger door, still gripping her arm hard. 'Get in.'

She got into the car. She had not struggled, she had not screamed. She didn't want to make trouble, she only

135

wanted to stop him from doing whatever insane thing he had planned. There was no one to help her, she would have to go with him, find out what was going on.

'What happened to your MGB?'

'I've sold it. Fasten your seat belt.'

'But why? Why would you do that?'

'I needed the money.'

Diesel glanced around her at the BMW's smart, clean interior. 'How did you get hold of this?' she asked, afraid she already knew the answer.

He gave her a scornful glance, 'How d'you think?'

'You stole it.'

'What if I did? Stupid berk had left a spare key in the glove compartment, all I had to do was get the door open. So, I took a car. So what. It doesn't matter any more.'

Diesel kept silent. The traffic was slow. The big white car edged onward through the narrow streets. They seemed to be heading for the ring road; heading out of town.

'I've never taken a car since I was fourteen and got into trouble,' said Jason, keeping his eyes on the traffic ahead. 'I've never stolen anything since then. I've never touched anything that I knew was stolen either. I know you don't believe that. Nobody believes it. Okay, maybe I don't pay National Insurance, I don't pay income tax. I don't *live* like that. It's all hand to mouth with me . . . Does that make me a criminal? Everyone in our neighbourhood thinks I'm a crook, whatever I do. Might as well make it true.'

Then he glanced down at the dashboard, and muttered something furious under his breath. Diesel looked too, and saw that the petrol gauge was resting on zero.

'I'm going to have to get some fuel. Stupid jerk who

owns this thing was running on empty. Are you going to sit quiet while I fill up?'

'I *told* you,' said Diesel. 'I don't want to get you into trouble. I want to help.'

The car slowed, they swung into the forecourt of a roadside garage.

'Stay where you are.'

The black sports bag was lying on the back seat. Diesel waited until he went into the shop to pay, then quickly dived over and pulled back the zip. He'd taken this bag into the dodgy pub, and come out with a face like death and thunder. Whatever wild plan was making Jason look so desperate, the explanation was in here ... There was nothing in the bag except a bundle of rags that smelt of motor oil. She picked it up, and felt something hard and heavy inside, some kind of tool? She pulled the rags apart, and gasped. It was a gun. A dark grey hand gun, with a black ribbed handgrip and a squat, compact barrel. A cold flood of shock went through her. She didn't have time to think, or to do anything but grab it, stuff it into her own bag, and zip up the sports bag again.

Jason got into the driver's seat without a word, and they drove off.

Diesel's head was spinning. That's why he sold his car, she thought. He sold his car to get the money to buy a gun. He sold his car to buy a gun, and he says he's going to do the only thing that will save Martin. How will a gun help? What can a gun do? Then the truth burst on her horrified mind. *He's going to kill someone.* She could taste something acid and disgusting in the back of her mouth, she thought she was going to be sick.

She remembered, as if it was something that had

happened in another life, Melanie from number 53 telling them the story of the Knight brothers: how Jason Knight had often been seen hanging around with real villains. So that was what he was going to do. He was going to kill a criminal, kill one of those dodgy friends, and then he would have *the body of a criminal who had died by violence.* Another dead body, to trade for Martin. Another dead body and guilty soul, to be taken over by the horrible zombie spell, so that Martin could go free. He's gone mad, she thought. Jason has gone completely mad.

Wild ideas rushed into her mind. Jason would take her with him to some criminal's house. The man would come to the door, and Jason would shoot him. Diesel would be forced to help him load the body into the back of the car, they would take it to the ruins, lay it in that haunted grave in the Abbey church. Then Jason would be a murderer, and it was all Diesel's fault. She was the one who had put the mad, horrible suggestion of finding *a better dead body* into his head. She tried desperately to think. At least she had the gun. He mustn't get it back. She must get rid of it. The gun was a terrible thing, she had to get rid of it. But how?

'I'm going to be sick.'

He was driving as fast as the law allows, out into the countryside. If they carried on this way they'd be passing through Browclough, passing the footpath to the Abbey. Where were they going? Must be out to some village retreat or lonely pub on the moors, where he knew he could find his victim. Jason glanced round. The way she looked must have convinced him she was telling the truth.

'If I stop, will you run off?' he asked.

'No! I don't want to run off. *I'm coming with you.*'

The BMW slowed and pulled up. Diesel jumped out,

grabbing her bag, and ducked into the bushes by the side of the road. She was back almost immediately, before he had a chance to come after her; holding a tissue to her mouth as if she'd really been sick.

'I'm sorry. I'm all right now.'

She had stuffed her bag into the branches of a bush, just out of sight. There'd been no time to hide it anywhere clever. She was terrified that he would notice she hadn't got the bag with her any more, but he didn't. He wasn't paying attention to her, or to anything.

Neither was Diesel. The next thing she knew, the BMW was pulling up again. She looked around her, the blood thumping in her ears, and was startled to see that they were in the layby near the path to the ruins. What were they doing here? Had Jason tricked his victim into coming out to the Abbey itself?

'Now this is where you stay in the car. I brought you because you wouldn't have kept quiet. If you couldn't get hold of the woman from the social, you'd have told your parents or called the police or something. But you're not coming any further.'

'What are you going to do?'

He didn't answer. He sat staring out of the windscreen, as if he couldn't bring himself to move. Diesel could hear a bird singing, serenading the warm summer evening as if there was nothing evil or unhappy in the world.

She'd been wrong. She was always getting things wrong about Jason. He hadn't planned to kill a living person. Jason wasn't a murderer. He'd bought the gun meaning to come out here with it, because he thought he could shoot the ghoul itself. *That* was how Jason had meant to release Martin from this horrible fate – by gunning down that shambling nightmare creature. She thought of the zombie with *strength as monstrous as its appetites*. It would be a good thing if it could be killed – if only it could be! Yet this monster was also *Martin*, or it had been Martin. Jason wasn't a murderer, but he had been going to kill his own brother!

'You're a good kid, Diesel,' said Jason. He didn't sound angry or crazy any more, just terribly tired. 'You really care, I know you do. I dunno, maybe you were the best thing that ever happened to our Martin. Pity things worked out the way they did. But it's no use crying over that. I'm the only one who can help my brother now. You've done everything a friend could do. Stay in the car. Give me half an hour, and then you can call your dad, or whoever you like, and get them to come and fetch you. Here's a phone. Call right now if you like. It doesn't matter. They can't get here in time to stop me.'

He'd taken a little cellphone from inside his jacket, he was trying to hand it to her.

'Is that stolen too?'

'You'd have to ask the lad I bought it from. I didn't bother. But it works.'

In her mind now, instead of Jason knocking on a door and shooting someone, she saw the shadowy ruins. Jason searching for the monster, and that undead creature leaping out at him with its terrible strength and speed, the bullets making no difference, the rending and tearing . . . But it wasn't going to happen. At least she'd prevented that.

'Jason. I know what you were going to do. You were going to try to kill that thing, that's why you bought the gun. But you can't kill it. It's dead! Bullets won't hurt it.

You'd have been killed yourself . . . It . . . he . . . Oh, it's too horrible, horrible.'

She had started to cry, pushing the phone away. Jason sighed, and put it on top of the dashboard. He leaned over to lift the black sports bag from the back seat: and then stopped, staring at her. 'What did you say?' he demanded. 'What do you know about a gun?'

Diesel shook her head, face buried in her hands. Jason grabbed the sports bag and ripped back the zip, searched inside, turned the bag upside down.

'Where is it!' he yelled, 'What did you do with it!'

'I d-don't know what you're talking about.'

She sat trembling, while he searched in vain under the seats and on the floor.

'Where's the gun?'

'Wh-what gun?'

'The garage!' he snapped, glaring at her furiously. 'No. You didn't get out at the garage. But it isn't in the car!'

'I th-threw it out of the window,' Diesel said. It was the only thing she could think of to say, to stop him before he reached the obvious explanation. 'I found it when you were paying for the petrol and I j-just threw it into the road when we were driving along.'

'No you didn't. I'd have seen that. Wait a minute. You felt sick. We stopped, because you were going to throw up. *That's* when you hid it!'

Too late, Diesel grabbed the doorhandle, meaning to jump out of the car and run. Jason slapped her hand away and shoved her back into the passenger seat, savagely hard. 'Oh no. You're coming with me. You hid it, you're going to find it for me.'

The BMW screeched in a tight circle and powered away, back towards the town.

They were through Browclough, racing along the country road on the other side, when the police siren started up behind them. Jason set his teeth, and floored the accelerator. But ahead of them, traffic was thickening. They were going to have to slow down, and then they would be caught. 'Hold tight,' he muttered, braked hard and slammed the big car around on its axis. Horns blared, but he was safely in the other lane, heading for the moors again at breakneck speed. 'I can lose them!'

'Jason, Jason, stop it! You can't do this!'

The same police car or another one was still behind them, siren yelling. Jason was gripping the wheel like a maniac. 'Slow down! Slow down!' screamed Diesel. The big truck, slowly crossing a little country junction ahead of them, reared up in front of her, rushing up on her like a great wall at the end of the universe . . .

Jason whacked through the gears, and swung the wheel. It was too late, there was no escape. They smashed into the wall.

The next thing Diesel knew she was lying in bed, and she was sleeping. There was no gap in her memory. She knew she had been in a car crash. She knew Jason had been driving a stolen car, and they'd been chased by the police, and they'd crashed into a truck. But no part of her was hurting. She wasn't even worried about Jason, because she was deeply asleep, lying quiet and still, surrounded by velvety darkness.

Martin came into the hospital room. He sat down on the end of her bed. She could feel him there, like the time before; like a real person, a real body.

'Hello Martin,' she whispered.

'Hi Diesel. Don't—'

'I know. I won't open my eyes.' But she reached out her hand, lifting it carefully because she had a feeling something was going to hurt a lot if she moved quickly. 'I wish I could touch you.'

'Better not.'

'Am I going to die?'

'No. You're not badly hurt. They'll let you go home soon.'

'Great,' she murmured, trying to smile. 'I'm *really* looking forward to talking to my parents about this, you can imagine—'

'They won't be too angry, just a bit because they were so scared. They love you.'

'I know. Martin?'

'Yeah?'

'Martin, you wouldn't come to me like this, if there was nothing I could do. You wouldn't be so cruel. I know you wouldn't be.'

The thing on the end of her bed moved a little. It sighed, thickly. In her mind's eyes she saw the monster: the sunken eyes, the grey skin, the teeth showing naked between lips tattered and oozing with decay. She kept her eyes tight closed and fought away the choking of disgust that rose in her throat.

'You know something that might help, and you're not telling me . . . because you're afraid to hope. Please tell me.'

'I'm almost gone, Diesel. I'm myself in your dream, but the real me is almost completely monster now. I can't tell you anything.'

'I know you can. Martin, you must try. Don't give up.'

143

'Well, okay. But what is it you think I can tell you?'

'It's the treasure, Martin.'

'What treasure?'

'You remember. Abbot Roger made a zombie to guard the Abbey's treasure. I told you about that. When the zombie got out of control, he reburied it in the church and tried to undo his spell. But we know that didn't work. According to the spell, the zombie was supposed to be with the treasure. Don't you remember, you said . . . when you woke up, when you started being the zombie, you thought you had to look for something? You were looking for the treasure, Martin.'

'I don't suppose it's there any more.'

'Maybe that doesn't matter. Maybe if we could get your body back to the secret place that would work. The zombie would be where it belonged, and you would be at peace.'

'Oh, I see. I mean, I think I see. But Diesel, the trouble is . . . I don't . . . I mean . . . it doesn't want to go back. This monster that I am wants to wander around, *it wants things*, it wants to hunt. Dunno how you'd make it climb back into the place it's supposed to be, and *sit and stay* like a good dog. I told you, there are no top magicians around these days. There's no expert you can call on.'

'I'll think of something. But Martin—'

She struggled to sit up. It did hurt, but she didn't care. She knew he was about to leave without telling her the most important thing.

'Did you find it? I think you did, you did! Where is the hiding place?'

She reached out. The creature that was half sitting, half crouched, on the end of her bed took shape, though her eyes were still closed. It gave a moan of horror and shame, and yet its loneliness was so great it almost leaned towards her, almost tried to take her hand.

But no. It couldn't be.

'No,' whispered Martin, 'Better not. Do you love me, Diesel?'

'Yes, I do.'

'Then you'll know.'

When she opened her eyes, she was alone. The hospital room was small and chilling and very real. But she remembered her dream. A nurse came in, and gently rearranged the pillows that had slipped from under her left arm, which was bandaged tightly from above the elbow to the wrist. She could feel more bandages round her chest.

'You're awake,' he said. 'You're parents are here, shall I let them in?'

Diesel's mum and dad came in, and stood looking down at her. When she saw the expressions on their faces she started to cry. For days and days she'd been thinking of them as the enemy, the people who kept getting in her way. Mum started crying too. She sat down on the chair by the bed. Dad took Diesel's right hand.

'Hi baby,' he said, tenderly. 'How are you feeling?'

'I'm all right.' She bit her lip and wished she hadn't, that hurt a lot. Her face was swollen and sore all over. 'What's going to happen to me? Will I have to go to prison?'

'No, darling,' said Mum. 'Someone from the police will want to talk to you, but there won't be anything to worry about. You'll come home with us, as soon as you're well enough.'

'What about Jason?'

'Jason is fine,' said Diesel's dad, grimly. 'He wasn't much hurt.'

'What about John? He was at home, alone—'

'John is fine too. Jason was conscious, he told them John was at home alone. The social services are taking care of him now, because they can't get hold of his mum.'

'But where's Jason?'

'Diesel,' said her mum gently but firmly, 'put it all out of your mind. If Jason and that truck driver hadn't both managed to swerve, you might have been . . . You might have been very seriously hurt. Don't think about anything that's going to worry you. You're coming home soon, where we can look after you, and you're going to rest and get well. Forget about other people's troubles.'

'I never thought I'd hear you say *that*, Mum,' whispered Diesel.

'Maybe I never had such good cause.'

Diesel had to give a statement. A woman police officer came to the hospital to talk to her. Diesel's mum stayed with her while the police officer asked questions. It wasn't difficult or frightening. She answered what she was asked. She didn't think it was wrong not to say things no one could possibly believe. She didn't mention the gun either, because she knew that would make things *much* worse for Jason. If it was wrong not to mention it, too bad.

It was strange that it had only been Sunday morning when she woke up in hospital. Ages and ages seemed to have gone by since she had sat on the rim of the Elephant Fountain, and seen Jason Knight passing in the street. She had cracked ribs, a greenstick fracture in one of the bones in her left forearm, and some spectacular bruises . . . The strong painkillers that the nurses gave her made her mind hazy. For the next two days she dozed through the hours, barely waking up to give her police statement; all the terrible truth at a distance, kept away from her by a layer of cotton-wool fuzziness. She could feel the challenge that Martin had given her working its way to the surface, from somewhere deep inside. It was like her ribs: too sore to be touched, but she knew she must think about it soon.

On Tuesday morning she felt much better. She was going to be allowed home. She'd have to stay in bed for a while; she planned to spend the time concentrating on being good to her mum and dad. Which was a funny way to put it, because they were the ones who were being so good to Diesel. But she meant to try and put her awful trouble out of her mind for as long as possible, for their sakes. Jason couldn't do anything crazy for the moment, and there was nothing she could do to help Martin until she could get up . . . She could tell how grateful they were that she was like their daughter again. It made her so ashamed. She'd been treating them as if they were strangers who hated her. It felt like coming back to life, to be friends with them again.

And then, suddenly, her brief escape ended.

She'd been moved into a normal ward. It was the middle of the morning. Diesel's mum, who had taken time off work to be with her, was sitting by her, reading to Diesel from one of her old favourite storybooks. A nurse came marching down between the rows of beds; not the nice man, but a stiff, cross-looking middle-aged woman. She whispered to Diesel's mum. Her mum got up, said 'Just a minute darling,' to Diesel, and went out with the nurse. A moment later she came back again, with another woman. It was Mrs Goodyear, the social worker who had been looking after Jason and John. Diesel's heart jumped. What was wrong *now*? Mrs Goodyear was looking flustered, anxious and shocked. She sat down on the other visitor's chair.

Diesel sat up sharply; which hurt her arm, and her cracked ribs.

'What's the matter?' she gasped. 'What's happened?'

'I'm afraid I've had some very worrying news, Diesel.'

Jason Knight had escaped from the young offender's prison, where he'd been taken to be 'held on remand' after the incident. 'I need to talk to you, Diesel,' said Mrs Goodyear, when she'd explained this. 'It's very, very important that you tell me all you know.'

'I didn't know Jason was in prison!' exclaimed Diesel. They'd told her he was in hospital too. 'He was hurt!'

'Only cuts and bruises. He'd been taken to Kinghall, that's the name of the young offenders' prison. He was in the sick bay. He's been missing since early this morning. It seems he simply climbed out of a window; a juvenile offenders' unit isn't exactly Alcatraz. Now, Diesel.' Mrs Goodyear looked grave. Diesel's mum took Diesel's hand. 'I have to talk to you about something very serious. The police believe Jason had bought a firearm, on the evening of the crash. They had a tip-off, they've followed it up, and there seems to be no doubt: he had a gun. The weapon wasn't in his possession on Saturday night, and it wasn't at the scene of the crash. Do you know *anything* about this, Diesel?'

'Oh *no*!'

'If you know anything, Diesel, you have to tell me. Jason

148

didn't have a record, except for that one incident when he was fourteen, and he's been looking after his younger brother very well. We could have made a good case for the fact that he only resorted to joyriding because he was deeply upset over Martin's death. But now things are much, much more serious. We must find him. If you care about Jason at all, you must not keep anything back. Do you know why he might have bought a gun? Do you know where he might have gone?'

Diesel's mum was looking horrified and bewildered. Diesel's mind was racing. What on earth could she say? 'I can't tell you anything,' she cried, bursting into tears. 'I don't know anything!' She fell back on the pillows, sobbing, shaking her head to and fro. 'Mum, make her go away, I can't stand to answer any more questions. It's too much, I can't stand it!'

The old ladies in the other beds were watching all this with great interest. Mrs Goodyear wasn't going to go on questioning a hysterical fourteen year old girl who was lying in a public hospital bed . . . Diesel went on crying until the social worker stood up with a helpless sigh. She was listening hard as Mrs Goodyear said, 'May I have another word with you, Mrs Prager'; and the two women moved away from the bed. But all she heard was Mrs Goodyear saying, 'I'm sorry I upset her. I'm just so *terribly* worried about Jason.'

In a few minutes, Diesel's mum came back. 'It seems like you're going to have to talk to the police again,' she said gently.

'But I don't know anything!'

'I know you don't, baby. You just never should have taken a ride with Jason Knight. And I blame myself, I was

149

the one who thought he was a good boy underneath it all . . . Don't worry, darling. I'm taking you home today. You'll feel better at home. Maybe tomorrow or the next day, you'll feel well enough to answer their questions. And your daddy and I will be there. We won't let any of these people bully you.'

She felt bad about putting on an act to deceive nice Mrs Goodyear, who had been so understanding and kind with Jason and John. But it couldn't be helped, she hadn't been able to think of any other way to behave. At least she had bought herself a little time.

After the doctor had seen her, and pronounced that all she needed now was a lot of rest, her mum helped her to dress and took her home in a taxi (Diesel didn't want any fuss. She had insisted she didn't need an ambulance). Soon she was in clean pyjamas in her own bed, sipping a cup of hot sweet tea. The weather had changed. Rain was streaming down from a dark sky outside Diesel's bedroom window, turning the summer afternoon into something like a winter evening. Diesel's mum brought out the storybook, and began to read.

Diesel had had to keep on being tearful and distressed for a while. It would have looked suspicious if she'd been suddenly calm again as soon as Mrs Goodyear left them. She was very glad to be back in her own bed again. She didn't have to put on an act any more. She could lie and stare at the ceiling and try to think, while her mother's soothing voice went softly on.

So the police knew that Jason had bought a gun. And Jason had escaped from prison. He'll have gone back to the place where he stopped to let me get out and be sick, she thought. He's got the gun again by now. She tried to tell herself he might not have found her bag . . . but there wasn't much chance of that. She could only hope that the crash had brought him to his senses: that he'd realised it was no use trying to kill the monster. But then why had he run away from the young offenders' unit? He'll have wanted to see John, she thought. Diesel knew John was staying in a social services place, until they'd sorted out who was going to look after him now. Poor John . . . Diesel's mum had told her where he was, and that he'd settled in okay; and that they could go and visit him, soon as Diesel was up and about. But would Jason know the address? He won't do *anything* until he's seen John's all right, she told herself. The Knight brothers stick together. That'll slow him down. Then when he sees John, he'll realise that he can't do anything crazy, because that would leave poor John-boy all alone . . .

Her thoughts went round and round, as she tried to convince herself that the worst, the most terrible things that might happen could still be prevented.

Something hit the windowpane, with a sharp crack.

Diesel's mum went on reading. She'd noticed nothing.

Another sharp, distinct crack; different from the sound of the rain . . .

'Mum,' said Diesel, 'I think I could go to sleep now.'

'All right dear,' said her mother, closing the book. 'I'll stay and sit with you quietly.'

'No, it's okay Mum. Go on downstairs, you deserve a break. I want to be alone and go to sleep.'

'All right darling.' Diesel's mum stood up, looking a little puzzled. She stroked back Diesel's hair from her forehead. 'I'll send your daddy up to you when he gets home. He won't be long now.'

She lay listening until her mum's footsteps had gone down the stairs, and the living room door had opened and closed. Then she got out of bed – all her bruises and her cracked bones zinging with pain – hobbled to the window and looked down. At first she couldn't see anything. Then she made out the white splotch of a face, peering up through the branches of those overgrown trees, in the garden next door. *You're crazy, Jason Knight*, she muttered to herself. '*You're hiding in the first place they'll look . . .*' She stood there, thinking; then crept over to her chest of drawers, trying not to make any painful moves, found a biro and a notebook and wrote, *Wait. I'll come down.* She tore the scrap of paper out of the notebook, and twisted it around a clip from her collection of hair slides to weight it down. It was tough work opening the window. Every muscle she owned seemed to be a new bruise. But she managed it, threw the message over the wall, and closed the window again.

Soon her dad came up. She lay there holding his hand and let him talk to her. When her mum came after him, with a mug of tomato soup and some bread and butter on a tray, she managed to eat. If her mum and dad noticed that she wasn't paying much attention to them, they didn't say anything. At last they left her alone.

Diesel listened and listened, until she was sure they were settled in front of the TV. Then she leapt up (and it hurt, but she didn't care) and hurried stealthily down the stairs, through the kitchen and out into the back garden; barefoot, in her pyjamas. Luckily the rain had stopped. She'd been wondering how on earth she was going to get over that wall, but there was no need. Jason was in the Pragers' garden, huddled against the back wall down by the greenhouse. He had no coat. He was soaked. The night wasn't cold, but he was shivering.

She stared at him, not knowing what to say. He handed her her daypack.

'Thought you'd want this.'

She grabbed the sodden bag, stupidly hoping the gun would still be inside. She could tell at once that it wasn't. 'Where's the gun?'

Jason smiled grimly, 'I've got it.'

'What are you doing here?' she whispered. 'This is the first place they'll look for you.'

'I had to see you were all right.' His white face was wet. She couldn't tell if that was rain, or if he was crying. 'I'm sorry for what happened to you, Diesel. I'm going out to the Abbey now . . . I won't see you again. You'll look out for our John, won't you.'

'Jason, you've got to give yourself up. They know about the gun, you're in dead trouble if you don't give yourself up.'

He shook his head. 'I know what I've got to do. No turning back.'

She knew she could not reason with him. He was too desperate, too wild in his misery; he was too far gone. All she could do was try to buy some time. 'Don't go there now,' she said. 'Wait until tomorrow. Wait until daylight. Then I'll come with you. I'm okay, I'm better. You can't be alone. You need somebody to help you.'

Jason laughed, a terrible sound; it was more like a cry of pain. 'You don't know what I'm going to do. You don't understand . . .'

'Yes I do. I *do*. I understand, you have to do whatever you can, to save Martin. I'll be there tomorrow.

Midday, at the ruined church. You be there too. Promise me.'

She didn't know what he planned, only that it must be something terrible. All she could do was try to make sure she'd be there to stop him. Jason stared at her in silence. She stared back, as bravely as she could. At last he nodded. 'Okay. I'll see you there.'

She managed to get back into the kitchen, and stuff the wet daypack out of sight, before she was caught by her dad. She told him she'd thought she could make herself a cup of tea without bothering them. He shouted at her for getting out of bed, but he shouted gently. He told her they weren't going to get tired of waiting on her hand and foot, not just yet. He put her back to bed and brought her the tea himself.

He could tell that she was hurting. She didn't argue when he told her to take some more of the pills she'd been given at the hospital, though she knew they would knock her out. Maybe it was the pills that made it easy for her to accept what was happening to her. To be calm and lie quietly, although she'd just been talking to a wanted criminal, in the rainy dark in her own back garden . . .

She slept well. When she woke, her mum was there with a mug of tea.

'Your dad's gone to work,' she said. 'It seemed a shame to wake you. He left your goodbye kiss with me.' She put down the mug and kissed Diesel. 'Now listen love, you're not to worry. You're not to get upset. I think they've probably got it all wrong about Jason and this gun. What would he want a gun for? He's never been involved in anything like that.'

'Has he been found?'

'Not yet. Not that anyone's told us, anyway. Don't worry about it. Now, what would you like for breakfast?'

'I'm feeling a lot better,' said Diesel. 'Could I have a fry-up? Bacon, beans, sausages, one of your terrific omelettes? And pancakes? The whole works?'

Her mum beamed in delight. 'Sure thing, babes. Coming right up!'

As soon as her mum as downstairs, Diesel jumped up. It *hurt*: but she really was feeling much better. She dressed as quickly as she could, ignoring the pain; choosing a long-sleeved shirt to hide her bandages. She looked in her mirror, to make sure the bandages were completely hidden. That's how she found out she'd better do something about her black eye and her swollen lip. But when she'd put on a bit of make-up the effect wasn't too bad. She tiptoed down the stairs. Her purse was in her daypack, in the kitchen, out of reach. She could hear mum in there, singing as she bustled about putting together the full breakfast works. Mum's coat was on one of the hooks in the hall. Feeling guilty but grimly determined, Diesel quickly searched the pockets, and took a fiver from her mum's wallet.

And then, out of the front door.

No note, no explanation . . . It was more painful than the bruises to think of mum happily cooking, and walking proudly into Diesel's room with her loaded tray; and finding it empty . . . I'm sorry Mum, she thought. I'm sorry Dad. But *this is an emergency*.

The place where John was staying wasn't far away, but she had to take a bus. It was a big house on the corner of a quiet street out in the suburbs, with its own walled gardens all around. It looked nice. But it was still the *Home* that poor John-boy had dreaded, the doom he had always feared. There were tall gates at the entrance, standing open. She was wondering if she dared to just go in, and ask someone for John Knight, when a dark blue minibus drove up, and went through the gates.

She followed it, and saw a group of children milling around at the front doors of the building, carrying school-bags. School! So much had happened, she'd forgotten all about school. But it was still termtime, in the normal world. It was a normal Wednesday morning.

The other children were talking and laughing, but John-boy obviously hadn't made any friends yet. He stood at the back as the others started piling into the bus. His school uniform was scruffier than anybody's else's, and he looked very anxious and pale. No one noticed a strange teenager, as she walked up to the group. Probably new faces were coming and going all the time. At first glance, she could easily have been someone living in this place. 'John!' she hissed.

He saw her and his eyes lit up. 'Diesel!'

There was no need to tell him what to do. He darted towards her. Next moment they were hidden in the trees that grew around the front lawns of the Home. The minibus drove off. The young care-worker who had been supervising disappeared back indoors.

'John, have you seen Jason?'

His anxious face broke into a grin. 'Jason's here! He came last night. You know what he did? He escaped from prison, to come and see me!' He looked at Diesel enviously. 'I know all about it. You were in the car, weren't you. It must have been really cool.'

'It was foul,' said Diesel, 'If that's "joyriding", you can

156

keep it. But what do you mean, *he's here*?' She could hardly believe it. 'Where? Is he here now?'

'He stayed last night. He's hiding. Come on, I'll show you.'

Trees and bushes grew all round the lawns and flower-beds of the big house. John led her, taking care to keep out of sight of the windows of the building, to a narrow space, like a tunnel roofed in branches, between the trees and the outer wall. He led her along this secret passage to where the branches of a big evergreen swept almost to the ground.

'Jason? Jason? Diesel's here!'

No answer. Together they ducked under the branches. There was a hollow in the ground, lined with copper-brown dead evergreen needles: and a damp, crumpled blanket.

'He's gone,' said John. All the cheerfulness went out of him. 'I brought him the blanket . . . I sneaked it out. Oh, I didn't think he'd go without saying goodbye.'

'What did he say to you, when he was here?'

John turned to her, biting his lip. 'He says I've got to stay here, Diesel. He says, he can't look after me no more. I mean, any more. He said he couldn't stay, that he'd be gone in the morning. But I thought he'd say goodbye!'

Diesel's left arm was aching like mad, and her cracked ribs hurt her every time she breathed. She put her hand on the hollowed-out bed, wondering if she could still feel a bit of warmth. Maybe he hadn't been gone long. She hoped, she *prayed* that when he got to the ruins, he would wait for her . . .

'Oh!' said John suddenly. 'Look! Look what he's left me!'

On a flat stone at the foot of the tree there was a little pile of possessions. A worn Swiss Army penknife, a penlight torch, a keyring with keys, a watch, a ballpoint pen shaped like a fish with purple scales, a purse, and a folded sheet of paper.

John picked up the paper and opened it.

For John-boy. Take care, our kid. Have a good life. Love, Jason.

'He must be coming back,' said John, uncertainly. 'He wouldn't have left me such good presents, if he wasn't coming back. Look, he's left me his Scorpio keyring. And his torch, and his money, and *his Swiss Army knife*! He never goes anywhere without that knife! Our dad gave it to him. He wouldn't give me presents if he was going to leave me all alone!'

Diesel felt a lump of coldness in her stomach, as if she'd swallowed a chunk of ice. She had a horrible feeling she knew, now, what it was Jason planned to do. She thought of him lying here, through the night, keeping watch over his little brother for one last time. She didn't think the presents meant that Jason was coming back. That wouldn't be possible. Not if he did what he meant to do, to set Martin free.

'John, we've got to go. You're going to miss school and get into trouble but I can't help it. We have to go after Jason. He needs us.'

'But where is he?'

'He's gone back to the ruins. Come on. There's no time to lose.'

'Shall I bring the presents?'

'Yeah, you bring them. Won't do any harm.'

The gates were still open, and they walked out without any

problem. They took a bus back to the town centre. John bought a chocolate bar and a drink at the bus station. Diesel couldn't eat or drink, she was too wound up. She was beginning to wish she'd brought some painkillers with her, but she hadn't so she would have to manage. Soon, though to Diesel it seemed that *hours* were rushing away, they were on the bus to Browclough. The sky was clear and bright above them as they walked along that familiar country lane. There were birds singing, and the trees and bushes were brilliantly green after the rain. Diesel half walked, half ran, limping where her bruises caught her, with John hurrying beside her, along the footpath to the Abbey ruins. One more time.

Five

They passed the old ticket booth, where a tarnished fivepence was still lying on the counter; and they were within the ruins. It was bright noon. The sun was high in a cloudless blue sky. In the distance, beyond the green towers of the lime avenue, the slopes of the moor, which had been dull brown when Diesel first saw this valley, had begun to turn purple with the blooming heather. A few sheep wandered, between the low stone walls.

'You stay here,' said Diesel. 'You keep watch, here by the entrance. I'll check the church.'

'I want to come with you,' said John. 'It's a bit creepy. I don't want to be left alone.'

'*No!*'

'What're you shouting at me for? I only said I want to come with you.'

'Well, you can't. Just *stay here*!'

'It's just that I don't like being on my own. This place is spooky.'

'No it isn't,' she snapped, near to breaking point. 'How can it be spooky in broad daylight? Nothing's going to happen. You stay there, I won't be long.'

She forced herself to walk, not run, across the bright turf.

Her heart was in her mouth, she was trembling with fear. If only she hadn't thought of that terrible idea . . . If only she hadn't put it into Jason's mind that Martin would be saved if they could bring to the ruins another *body of a criminal, who had died in violence* . . . It was Diesel's fault, Diesel was to blame for the terrible thing that Jason planned to do. Not to shoot the ghoul. That wasn't why he'd wanted the gun. It wasn't the ghoul he'd decided to kill.

It was himself.

She reached the gap in the west of the ruined church, hardly able to make herself put one foot in front of the other, terrified of what she would see.

Jason was sitting on one of the table tombs, with his head bowed. The black sports bag was lying at his feet. The dark pit of Martin's grave, open once more, was a few metres away. She felt weak with relief. But she knew the battle wasn't over. As she came closer he looked up, but he didn't move. The wild desperation that had been in his face, when he was hiding in the Pragers' back garden, was gone. He was calm. But it was a frightening calm; as if nothing mattered.

'Hi Diesel,' he said. 'I knew you'd come. You're a brave girl.'

'You mustn't do it,' she whispered.

His arms were folded, his right hand hidden inside his leather jacket. 'Don't make it harder for me, Diesel. You said you knew what I was going to do. You said you understood.'

Diesel was crying, tears running down her face. She couldn't stop them. 'I know what you were going to do, Jason. I know why you got the gun. It was my stupid idea about giving the spell another body to work on.'

'Yeah. A criminal who died by violence. In trade for our Martin.'

'I understand, I understand! But it's *wrong*!' she sobbed. 'Please, please listen to me.'

'Yeah,' he went on, with bleak satisfaction, ignoring her. 'I can provide the goods. Dead easy. No need to go "robbing the police morgue". That was a terrible, stupid idea, I'm surprised at you. I fit the bill, I'm here, I'm willing. I'm going to put myself in Martin's place. I shifted the stone. Got some tools out of our garden shed last night, brought them with me. You'll have to try and get the stone back in place, after. Doesn't matter if you can't, though. No one comes here. And after I've been in there a night, it won't make any odds.'

Diesel wiped her eyes, and tried to steady her shaking voice. 'Jason, listen to yourself. This is all c-c-crazy. Anyway, you're not a criminal!'

'Yes I am. I nearly killed you the other night, driving in a car I stole. Don't tell me you don't remember?'

She didn't know how to talk to him, how to reach him. He was out of his mind. The rush of relief that had swept through her, when she saw he was still alive, had turned to a flood of panic and despair. She had to get the gun away from him, but she didn't know how.

'I remember, yes I remember,' she babbled. 'But that doesn't make you . . . a bad person. You *can't do this*, Jason. It's horrible, it won't do Martin any good. How can it help him, to have you dead?'

'Don't come any nearer, Diesel. That's close enough.'

She saw his eyes change. Snap, like that time in the street before he grabbed her. Like a light going out. Like a switch flicking from on to off. She knew that in his mind he had already pulled the trigger. In his mind he had passed the point of no return. 'Seems like I had to wait for you,' he said, in that mad, dead-calm voice. 'I needed someone to be here. But I can do it now.' He took his hand out from his jacket; it was holding the gun. He lifted it to his head . . .

'No!' wailed Diesel, flinging herself forward.

But her bruises and her bandaged arm made her clumsy. It wasn't Diesel who stopped him. As she tried to grab his arm, Jason gave a groan. His mouth opened in horror and the hand with the gun in it dropped. Diesel grabbed for the gun. She only managed to knock it out of his hand. It landed, spinning, on the ground, right beside the over-turned stone with that fatal inscription, NON LICET PERTURBARI. She dived for it, but Jason got there first. In a moment the gun was hidden again inside his jacket: and they both stood there, looking at the boy who had appeared in that great gap in the western wall.

'You shouldn't have done it, Diesel,' muttered Jason, furiously. 'I *trusted* you.'

'Jason!' John came running up. His eyes were huge with excitement in his pale face. 'Jason! You've got a gun!'

'No I haven't,' snapped Jason. 'Don't be stupid. What would I be doing with a gun?'

'I *saw* it,' insisted John. 'What's the gun for, Jason? Is it real?'

Jason was glaring at Diesel. 'That was a dirty trick, bringing John. I'd said goodbye to him. I left him every-thing I had to give him: I know it wasn't much. Why'd you have to bring him?'

She wiped her eyes, her voice was still shaking. 'I d-don't care. It worked.'

'You haven't stopped me. I'm going to do it. You're

going to take John away, and I'm going to do it. I won't turn back now.'

'What are you talking about?' demanded John. 'Why's Diesel all upset? I'm not going to be taken away. I know what the gun's for. You're going after the thing that took Martin.'

'Never mind what I'm doing. You are going home. I mean, back to that nice foster place. With Diesel. Right now.'

'Yeah,' said Diesel, furiously. 'You're *going into care*, John-boy. The worst thing you ever thought could happen, after Martin died. You're going to be all alone. Because Jason is going to *abandon you* and let that happen, and you're never going to see him again.'

'He'll be better off,' said Jason. 'I'm no good to him, or anyone.'

John looked from one of them to the other, completely bewildered.

If only she had understood before this, thought Diesel, how much Jason cared. She'd been afraid of his reputation, and offended at the way he treated her like a stupid kid. She had not seen how desperately he was struggling to deal with the truth about Martin . . . Now at last she understood. Maybe it was too late, but at least *she understood*. Anger at Jason, and at herself for her stupidity, made her strong; gave her the will to stop crying and fight.

'I won't let you say that! You are *not* no good! I know how much you loved Martin, but don't you care about John? He needs you!'

Jason shook his head. 'Get out of here and take him with you.'

'Listen, you *don't have to do this*! There's another way.

164

The thing was supposed to stay and guard the treasure. My idea about getting another body was stupid and mad. What we need to do is to somehow get the thing back to its proper place. Then it will sleep, and Martin will be at peace. I even think I know where the hiding place must be. It's that name, the name *The Boatman*, that's the clue . . .'

It was no use, she could see she wasn't getting through to him.

'You and your bright ideas,' sneered Jason. 'Bright ideas don't work, Diesel. The world isn't like that. Give it up.'

'Are we going treasure hunting?' asked John, catching at something that sounded positive.

'Yes!' said Diesel. 'That's it. We're going treasure hunting. The gun isn't a real gun, it's a fake one. Jason was going to use it to scare those enemies of his. *Now he's going to give me the fake gun.* And we're going treasure hunting, all of us.'

'I am not going to give you the gun,' said Jason. 'Let me do what I have to do.'

'Well then, I'm going treasure hunting by myself. John, you stay with Jason. Maybe he'll let you play with his new toy.'

'Oh yeah!' exclaimed John. 'Let me see it, Jason!'

Diesel drew a deep breath. She turned her back and walked away. It felt like the worst, riskiest thing she had ever done in her life. But it would work, if John stayed with Jason. She glanced back once, then she resolutely kept on walking. The sooner she was away from here the better. Jason couldn't do anything terrible, not while John was alone with him.

She'd passed through the gap in the west wall, when she

heard footsteps behind her. John had caught up, panting. 'He says I've got to come with you,' he said miserably.

Diesel whirled around . . . It was too late. The ruined church was empty.

'Oh no!' moaned Diesel. 'Where has he gone? John, you should have stayed with him!'

'But we always do what Jason tells us,' said John blankly, as if Diesel must have known this. '*Always*, me and Martin. We have to. He's all we've got.'

Diesel grabbed John's hand. 'We've got to find him! Come on!'

'Aren't we going treasure hunting?' demanded John.

'No, we're going Jason-hunting. Come on!'

John was resisting. She tugged at his hand.

'Look,' cried John, 'There he is! Over there!'

She looked the way he was pointing, in time to see a man-sized shadow slip out of sight behind a pillar of stone, further into the ruins. John twisted his hand free and started to run, crying, 'Hey, Jason, Jason!'

For a moment Diesel could not move. The sky was blue, the sun was high. But it was like her dream, her first dream . . . a darkness in the sunlight, a black, bitter cold under the warmth of the day. It had only been a glimpse, but *she knew what she had seen.*

The ghoul had been growing stronger and hungrier. Now it roamed by daylight.

She ran after John, and caught up with him at the opening of a passageway where the ruined walls on either side stood taller than most, though it was open overhead to the blue sky. The passage led towards the entrance of the great kitchen. John was standing as if paralysed. At the end of the passage someone was peering at them, from behind a wall.

It was not Jason. It was something . . . that wasn't human any longer.

Diesel could not look too closely. The details were very ugly.

'It's . . . looking . . . at . . . us,' John said, in a cracked whisper.

The thing came fully into view, slightly stooping, its hairless head pushed forward. It took a couple of loping, shambling strides. Diesel grabbed John again, and they ran.

They ran towards the church. But Diesel knew there would be no shelter there from evil, the holy ground was contaminated. She veered away, hauling John with her. They stumbled hand in hand, hurrying between the lumps of ruined wall, and dived into the foundations of the scriptorium, the surviving undercroft of the place where the old monks used to copy manuscripts. It was a big place, sunken below ground level, the floor divided by low stone bulwarks.

'What are we going to do?' wailed John. 'We'd better find Jason, he's got the gun!'

'I don't think the gun's any use,' gasped Diesel, not bothering to tell him again that the gun was a toy. 'But we've got to find Jason. Let me think!'

John gave a whimpering moan.

The creature had found them. It was peering into the sunken room, its tattered face pale against the grey stones. 'Up the wall!' gasped Diesel. 'Quick! Up the wall!' She pushed John ahead of her and dragged herself after him, one arm half-useless, her cracked ribs and all her bruises stinging and aching. The thing was right behind her. John was at the top of the wall. *It can't be real*, she told herself, *ghosts aren't solid like that*. Ghosts are vapour, ghosts are

167

mist and shadows . . . In her hours of lonely fear, and out here at night, she had believed in the ghoul. In daylight, in bright sunlight, the thing that was at her heels seemed utterly impossible. It could not exist!

But it did.

She yelled to John, 'Go on! Get away!' He disappeared. A clammy touch, like the grip of a foul wet dishcloth, had fastened on her left ankle. She was surrounded by the smell of something long dead. She kicked out. The dishcloth touch kept clinging on; she kicked again, grabbing frantically for the top of the wall. She was free. She flung herself over into soft grass.

'What are we going to do?' cried John, 'What are we going to do?'

'I know . . . I know what . . . We're going to bury it! . . . Come on!'

All Diesel's bruises had stiffened up, and her left arm felt as if it was on fire. But she knew where she was heading: the place she wanted was in the big kitchen. She was afraid it would be too clever, that it wouldn't follow but get ahead of them and lie in wait. But when she deliberately showed herself, in the open between two rows of low, wall-stumps, *it was there*. She saw the red, sunken eyes as it came trotting, like a hunting animal, towards her. *It isn't a person*, she realised. *It doesn't think like a person* . . . And that knowledge filled her with both horror and relief. She remembered Martin's voice, in her dream saying, 'I am almost gone, I am almost this monster', and gave a sob. But there was no time for grief. She grabbed John's hand again and they ran into the kitchen.

'Here,' gasped Diesel. 'Up here!'

In the wall by the big chimney where the bats roosted,

there was the remains of a spiral stairway which had once led to the floor above. It was now just a couple of turns of stone steps that ended in a pile of loose rubble. One of those rusty signs, relics of the time when the Abbey was open to visitors, was fixed to the wall beside it, warning: DANGER DO NOT CLIMB. Diesel and John went up the narrow steps like two frantic rockets, and scrambled together over the insecure heap of stone and debris at the top. In front of them was the open space of a long-ago window, with a drop of about three metres down to the ground. They stood, panting, clutching onto each other's hands, and turned back to see what was happening. The monster was in the kitchen. Its head nodded to and fro. It seemed to sniff around, and then it darted, silently, with horrible speed, to the broken stairway.

'Not yet!' whispered Diesel.

John was clinging to her wrist so hard it felt as if his nails were drawing blood. 'Diesel . . .' he said, 'Are we awake? Or is this a nightmare? Are we in a nightmare?'

'Sssh!'

The thing was at the foot of the stairs, peering up. She saw the gleam of its naked teeth.

'Don't look at it. *Don't look at it*, John! Just shove! Now!'

She sobbed, and thrust with all her weight against the pile of rubble. It gave way with a rumble and a crash; and Diesel and John leapt together out of the window.

They rolled over and crouched in the grass. Diesel put her head in her hands, gritting her teeth to stop herself from wailing in pain. No sound from the kitchen behind them.

'Is it done for?' demanded John. 'Oh Diesel, I'm sure

we're in a nightmare. We can't be awake. *I saw its face*. Its face looked like, I don't know, I daren't say!'

'Hush,' she said. 'Come on. We've still got to find Jason.'

Diesel held John's hand again, as she led him to the lime avenue.

How well she remembered that first day when Martin had brought her here: the sunlight, the great trees still barely clothed in spring green. She remembered telling him that this was a *Linden Grove*, and seeing his face fall: the last thing he'd wanted was to be reminded of his life at home. I was always saying the wrong thing, she thought. Always getting things wrong . . . She just hoped she was right this time. But she felt sick with dread, in case she wasn't. The place on her ankle where the ghoul's hand had gripped her was numb and sore. It was buried, but she knew they'd only slowed it down. You can't kill a monster that is already dead.

'Where are we going?' came John's frightened voice.

'It's under this archway. You know this place. Martin's place.'

The trees rustled overhead. They ducked under the low arch. 'Get out that penlight,' said Diesel. Diesel first and then John, they climbed down under the earth, into the darkness. The thin beam of torch light danced over earth floor and walls; there was a sound of moving water.

'I know what this is,' cried John. 'He never brought *me* here, but he told me about it. It's Martin's secret cave!'

'Yes,' said Diesel. Soon they had reached the cave itself, with the canal running through it, and that column of white sunshine falling from above, casting shadows of light on the dark water. Diesel sat down. She wrapped her arms around her knees, and dropped her head onto them, unable to stop the tears. Martin's secret place . . .

'Diesel!' John tugged at her shoulder. 'Diesel, Diesel, get up! *There's something moving!*'

He was right. Something was moving, by the wall of the cave where it sloped down to the water. The penlight beam caught the movement, but not much more. John wailed. 'Oh no! How did it get here ahead of us? We buried it!'

If that was the ghoul, they were finished. Diesel knew she could not run another step. She could not fight. The most she could hope was that John would have a chance to get away . . .

Suddenly they were both blinded by a brilliant splash of light.

'I told you two to go home,' said Jason.

He was kneeling by the wall, staring at them through the beam of a big flashlight. His face was very pale. Behind him, there was a darkness on the darkness . . . For a moment Diesel couldn't make out what she was seeing. Then she realised there was a hole in the wall. A hole in the wall of the cave, an utterly black space beyond.

'Did you do that?' she cried.

'No. Not much of it. Something's been down here, digging. I finished it off.'

Diesel clambered to her feet and limped across to him. She looked at the ancient, rotten brickwork, that had been uncovered behind the earth wall of the cave. Jason had pulled out several of the crumbling bricks.

'Oh, cool,' breathed John. 'The treasure place!'

'I was going to lie down in that grave,' said Jason, in a dreamy, wondering tone of voice. 'The grave with the stone that said Do Not Disturb. But I disturbed it.'

171

'Lie down in the grave?' repeated John, 'Wh-what for?'

Jason took no notice. 'But this is better. You said "The Boatman is the clue," Diesel, and then I knew. It comes here, Diesel. You were right, it is drawn to this place, where the treasure was buried. It couldn't get inside, because the way in was bricked up and buried. But it'll come back. When it does, it will find me. And then I'll do what I have to do. I couldn't save our Martin's life, but *I can save his death*. I can take his place.'

'What are you talking about?' demanded John.

Diesel had collapsed onto the floor again, nursing her bandaged arm. Jason sounded as if he was in another world, a terrible dream-world. She could only pray he wouldn't actually turn the gun on himself in front of John. But where *was* the gun? He wasn't holding it. She could see his jacket, lying on the ground. If the gun was in his jacket . . .

'What have you found, Jason? Let's see what you've found.' As she spoke she got up and limped forward, and John came with her. But all her attention was on that jacket.

He let them come closer. All three of them together peered through the hole. Behind the bricks, John's penlight showed a hollow space like a little room. Inside this room, almost filling it, was something that had once been a boat. Maybe it had been used on the canal. Diesel could make out a curve of clinker-laid planks, some completely collapsed, some kept together by a thick coating of tar. In the bottom of the boat there were three small chests, and an irregular lump that might be a bag of some kind. In the space beyond the chests there was room as if for someone to sit and row the boat, but nobody was sitting there now.

Jason raised the big flashlight. He pushed until some more of the rotten bricks gave way, reached in and groped at the lumpy bag, which crumbled at his touch; and brought his hand out filled with some of the bag's contents.

They all moved back, and Jason opened his hand. The palm was full of flat round things. They were coins. Some of them were tarnished black, some of them gleamed yellow.

'Oh, wow!' gasped John. 'We found the Abbey treasure!'

Jason laughed. 'We're rich,' he said. 'We're rich. You can have all the pizza you can eat, John-boy. You can have whatever you like. All our dreams can come true! Martin . . . Martin can have his Jensen Interceptor!'

'That's great,' said Diesel, reaching out one hand for the leather jacket, speaking as calmly as she could. 'We found the treasure. Now everything's going to be okay. But Jason, you've got to get John away from here. The ghoul is out by daylight. It chased us.'

'Why does he have to take me away?' said John. 'I want to help fetch out the treasure. We don't have to worry about that thing. We *buried* it, Jason. We did for the ghoul!'

'I don't think so,' said Diesel. She was glad John had forgotten the glimpse he'd had of the monster's face. He was only twelve. The truth was too bad for him to bear. 'I don't think we killed it. You can't kill something that's dead. We slowed it down. But I think it will follow us here, and then I know what to do.'

'She's right,' said Jason. 'You can't kill the evil. You can only do a deal with it. But that's my job, not yours, Diesel. *You* take John, and get out.'

She had hold of the jacket. She dragged it towards her and fumbled in the pockets. *There was no gun.* 'You go with Diesel now, John,' said Jason. 'You go home.'

'No!' cried Diesel. 'No! We won't leave you! Jason you can't—'

Behind them, something that had been crawling down the passageway reached the entrance to the cave; a thing like an animal, crawling on the ground: a head naked of hair, a lipless mouth, sunken eyes that gleamed red. John-boy heard the movement, looked around and screamed. The creature stood upright, its loose-jointed arms swinging. Diesel's mouth was making *no, please no* without a sound. The monster took no notice of her, or of John. It flung itself at Jason in a deadly, silent rush; grabbed him by the throat; began to shake him violently from side to side. Its lipless mouth was open in a snarl; the foul smell of something long dead filled the air . . .

'Let him go! Let him go!' shrieked John. He'd dropped the penlight. The wide beam of the flashlight swung wildly as it flew out of Jason's hand, and landed on the floor. John and Diesel heard Jason's gasping breath, as the creature threw him up against the wall of the cave. *It is going to bite his throat out*, thought Diesel.

'Drop the coins!' she yelled. 'It's attacking you because you're taking the treasure! *Drop the coins!*' She cast wildly around for a weapon, grabbed a rotten half-brick, lunged forward . . .

But the brick fell from her hand.

She had no strength left. But if she had been strong it would have been no use. She could not strike. Through the flickering shadows that meshed the two struggling bodies, she saw that Jason had got one hand free. He was pulling the gun out of the waistband of his jeans, where it had been hidden. His hand came up, he was trying to press the muzzle against his temple . . .

'No!' wailed Diesel, despairingly. 'Jason, *please*!'

John was huddled back in the darkness, sobbing frantically.

But Jason did not fire. Something stopped him. Was that a choking whisper, rising from the throat of the dead thing? No, please, surely the monster couldn't have spoken its brother's name . . .

Jason's hand dropped, the gun fell. The thing had let go of his throat. It stood, swaying, uncertain . . .

Diesel crawled over and grabbed the weapon, and stuffed it in her pocket. 'Put the coins back,' she whispered, 'Put them *back*.' She saw Jason pick up the coins that had been shaken from his hand, she saw him reach through the hole to replace them inside the boat. Still the monster stood and swayed. 'Every one of them,' breathed Diesel . . . and a last gleam of gold revealed itself, on the edge of the torchlight. Jason picked it up, and returned it to the hoard.

The creature still waited.

Diesel had tried to prepare herself for this moment. But she couldn't move.

In her dream, Martin had said, *it's no use, you'll never find a magician these days*. But magic hadn't worked for Abbot Roger, when he tried to break his own spells. Maybe magic wasn't what was needed. I know what to do, thought Diesel suddenly. I need to shut my eyes. Then it will be easy. She closed her eyes, praying *please God, let this be right*. Eyes tightly shut, she stood and reached out through darkness.

She found herself holding someone's hand.

Don't open your eyes, and it's like the world doesn't exist.

Only you and me, Martin. Only you and me . . .

She could not bear to think of what the hand would look like if she could see it, but the darkness protected her. Something protected her, too, from the horror of feeling that *this was Martin*. All she felt was a great pity, for the poor dead body and the spirit trapped within it, taken over and misused by the old magician's worthless magic.

Abbot Roger had chosen to trade goodness for the power of magic, and the exchange had betrayed him. Diesel had no choice. There was nothing she could do but pray. She had no other power. She held the creature's hand, and prayed to God that it should rest in peace.

'Now you are safe,' she murmured. She didn't know if it could hear or understand, but it seemed right to speak. 'Be quiet, rest now. Go to sleep, the real sleep, the long sleep. That old, rotten magic will let you go. The spell is really broken this time. Be at peace.'

The hand she had been holding slipped out of her grasp. She heard a shuffling, a scrabbling of animal movement, and opened her eyes to see the grey figure clambering through the hole in the wall of the hiding place. There was a little more scuffling. Then there was silence.

'*Martin?*'

This time she did not know if she had spoken aloud or silently. But she felt that something touched her. As the monster, released from living death, settled in its resting place, *something touched her*. A breath, a sigh, a sweetness that flew away and was gone: a last goodbye. Diesel dropped to her knees. She knew she was crying, but she couldn't even feel the tears on her face. She heard Jason give a great sob. She saw him stumble forward, and begin thrusting handfuls of brick and earth into the gap in the hidden wall.

'Bury it, bury it!' she heard him gasp.

Then something heavy shifted, and suddenly, with a muffled roar, the whole cave seemed to be moving. John shrieked, 'Diesel!' Earth was falling on her like heavy rain. There was earth in her mouth, on her eyes . . . They were all three going to be buried, along with the treasure and its guardian. She tried to struggle but she couldn't; and everything went black.

Don't open your eyes.

But slowly, reluctantly, she finally did open her eyes.

She was lying on the ground, out in the warm, bright air. It hurt to breathe. Jason and John were kneeling beside her, looking down anxiously into her face.

'Diesel?' said John. 'Are you all right? The cave fell on you. We had to drag you out.'

'I'm all right.'

'We lost both the torches, and the treasure's buried again,' said John.

'It can stay buried,' said Jason. 'We don't want it.'

'Yeah!' agreed John. 'I don't care, as long as *that thing* is buried too.'

'It doesn't matter,' said Diesel. 'It's harmless now. The spell is broken.'

All three of them were silent, for a short while. Then Diesel carefully sat up. Both the brothers put their arms around her.

'I think we've been in a nightmare,' said John. 'We've been in a nightmare, and we're out of it now. We're back in the real world . . . where things like *that* don't happen. And it's all gone. It isn't real any more. It's like all that stuff about the ghoul and everything never was.'

'Come on,' said Jason, 'Let's go. It's time to take Diesel home. Time for the Knight brothers to face the music.'

He helped Diesel to her feet. The three of them walked away through the ruins. Diesel turned back, once more, at the old ticket booth. But there was no sense of presence, nothing that haunted her. Only the crumbling stones, lonely but peaceful in the quiet sunlight.

The Knight boys faced the music. Jason was in real trouble, but the fact that Diesel had brought the gun back, and it had not been fired, was a good thing. Mrs Goodyear stood up for him valiantly, and he didn't get a custodial sentence. He wouldn't be parted from John. A few weeks after that day in the Abbey ruins, he came round to tell Diesel that he and John were moving out. They were moving to a flat the social services had found for them, a smaller place, easier to look after and near to where their mum was living. They'd agreed to see their mum sometimes. She'd moved out of the boyfriend's place, and wanted to try and start again.

'It won't work,' said Jason. 'But what can you do? You can't say no.'

They didn't talk about Martin, or what had happened in the ruins. None of that. Those were secrets that were buried deep, and would stay buried, like Abbot Roger's treasure.

'We'll keep in touch,' said Diesel. 'You and me and John. I'm not going to give up on you two. I'm going to be your friend. Forever.'

'Yeah,' said Jason. 'We'll keep in touch.'

They both meant it. But time would tell.

Diesel's broken arm needed a cast and her ribs took ages to heal after the additional battering she'd given herself. It took her all summer to recover. But by autumn she was completely better, and she'd stopped having nightmares. One day in October, when Jason and John had moved out, she sat on the front wall of number 57 after school, and watched the new people moving into number 55. The big pieces of furniture had been carried into the house by the removal men. Now the family were unloading cardboard boxes and carrier bags full of their most precious possessions from their car. There were two children. One was a boy about six years old. The other was a girl of Diesel's age. She was a white girl, thin and tall. She had long, shiny light-brown hair, tip-tilted green eyes and a very pointed chin. She looked rather strange, but interesting. On the way into the house with one of those cardboard boxes, she stopped and stood, looking straight at Diesel with her mermaidish green eyes. She didn't speak, but she nodded slightly; as if to say, Yeah. Maybe we will like each other.

So life goes on, thought Diesel, that night as she changed into her pyjamas.

Life goes on, and there are no ghouls in my dreams. Nothing frightening in my days.

Nothing is wrong with my world. Except that Martin's dead.

She picked up Herbie the squirrel, who had fallen on the floor, and propped him back in his usual place by her pillow. Then she sat on the bed, and leaned her cheek against the wall, with her eyes closed and the tears falling quietly.

Listening for the radio.

Other books by Ann Halam

The Powerhouse

'The face looked at Maddy. I saw its empty eyes gleam . . . Somebody screamed and screamed. I think it was me.'

Robs, Jef and Maddy: three friends who just wanted to make music together. How could one summer change their lives the way it did? Maddy and Robs survived, but only just. And the nightmare that happened in the Powerhouse will live with them forever.

'superbly packaged horror' *Books Magazine*

'worth twenty Point Horrors' *School Librarian*

The Fear Man

A dreadful secret hangs over the house in Roman Road. What is it that keeps drawing Andrei to it? And what is the unknown presence that seems to be stalking the family? Constantly on the run from a father he has never known, Andrei is living a nightmare. A compelling story of vampires, magicians and creatures of darkness.

'brilliantly written . . . a very powerful and affecting book' BBC Radio 4 *Treasure Islands*

The Haunting of Jessica Raven

'*Darkness. A cold, foul-smelling darkness. Some-where a child was screaming.*'

Mysterious thing start happening to Jessica when, on holiday in France, she meets a group of ragged children. She cannot work out where they come from, but when she meets their leader, an older boy called Jean-Luc, she begins to realise that they may hold the key to her brother's fatal illness.

'a novel of singular completeness and perfection. With it Ann Halam confirms her standing as one of the most exciting of emerging talents' *Junior Bookshelf*

Crying in the Dark

'*She didn't know why she had such a strange feeling that they shouldn't have left her alone – but suddenly she understood what the ghosts were trying to tell her. She could make the Madisons wish they'd never been born . . .*'

Bullied and abused by her adoptive family Elinor retreats into the restless, vengeful past that haunts their seventeenth-century home. At first it's a way to escape, but soon she's a prisoner and the price of her freedom is something too terrible to contemplate.

'An excellent and compelling ghost story' *The Guardian*

The N.I.M.R.O.D. Conspiracy

'*Dear Mum – I'm wedged under the sea-defences, most of me has been eaten by the fishes. Love, Stacey.*'

Stacey vanished three years ago. She's dead. It's Alan's fault. He knows. But Mum refuses to believe it – her endless search for her little daughter leads them first to NIMROD, and then into a criminal underworld of deceit and conspiracies, burglary, blackmail and terrible danger. NIMROD wields a mysterious power. But *who* are they really? What do they know about Stacey? What can they possibly want from Alan and his mum?

'a chilling, exciting story' *Our Schools Magazine*